The Periwinkle Turban

The Periwinkle Turban

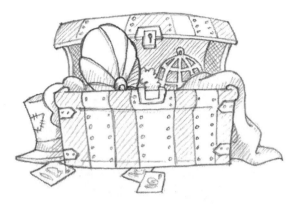

Matthew Mainster

Illustrations by Lindsey S.M. Loegters

Lee Press

U.S.A

Lee Press

First Paperback Edition: October 2012

ISBN-13: 978-0615701967
ISBN-10: 0615701965
Library of Congress Number: 2012917963

10 9 8 7 6 5 4 3 2 1

Printed in the United States of America

To Mary, for giving us Isabelle
To Isabelle, for giving us Jane
To Jane, for giving us Lea
and
To the last three for loving me

Table of Contents

In Which We Meet
The Swopes

Now dear readers, let us first brush up on our British accents before we begin, for the children in this book were quite British, and their story will sound very silly indeed if spoken with any other accent. If you're not sure how to speak with a British accent, try asking your parents to demonstrate one for you. Not all parents are skilled in these matters however, and they may sound as though they're speaking with mashed potatoes in their mouths. If you find this to be the case, you're best to ask a nanny instead, for any proper nanny is almost always British and usually very helpful with these sorts of things.

Now that we have that settled, let me start by telling you the names of the Swope children. They were Everett,

Charles, and baby Isabelle. As I said, they were British, and they wouldn't have wanted you thinking otherwise simply because they lived in America. This is not to say that they did not like their home in Maryland (that's pronounced "mare-uh-lind" and not "mary-land" they had discovered), but as British citizens by birth, their loyalty was first and foremost to the King, of course. You might be wondering what King I speak of. I shall tell you that it was King George the Fifth. You won't have heard of him on the news or seen him waving on palace balconies with the rest of the royal family because he has long since been dead. Dead, dead, dead. But in 1920 he was very much alive, and it is in this year that our story begins.

Now, (have you noticed that's the third time I've started a paragraph with the word "now"? It does pain me to do it, but I assure you it couldn't be helped) ... Now, since it's very tiresome when books stop to tell you all the characters ages and occupations just as things were starting to get interesting, I'll get it over with straightaway.

Everett and Charles Swope were eight and seven years-old respectively, though Everett was quick to remind Charles that he was much nearer to nine than eight, while Charles, on the other hand, would be seven a great deal longer. They also had a baby sister named Isabelle, but she was much less fun to play with considering she was still of the age at which one is contained within cribs and strolled around in perambulators.

Their mother's name was Mary, though they had only ever heard her called this from across the dinner table when their father required her to pass the salt. Otherwise, she was known as "Mum", and Charles and Everett were ever so lucky for it, for she was very kind-hearted, and always made the best after-school pudding. And as Everett once said, she never put up a fuss when one of their trousers needed mending, which in the summertime was quite a lot.

Their father certainly must have had a name as well, I suppose, but the children weren't quite sure of it. He'd come from one of those aristocratic families that saw fit to christen their male children with the names of at least the last four generations of grandfathers. So his name was Wallace Edward Arthur Lawrence, or Edward Lawrence Arthur Wallace, or something of the like, but around the house he was never called anything but "Father". And a good father he was — genial, loving, and mild tempered. He was seldom stern, but when the occasion did occur, Charles and Everett often felt they quite deserved it and were nearly always compliant with their father's punishments.

Father was a grocer by trade, and he owned the grocery store at the front of their house. The children suspected he was rather well off, though they didn't let on about this to the other children in the neighborhood because they doubted it would be very polite. But it should be known that the Swopes were never wanting for new clothes or pencils and schoolbooks, and not many other families in Coopstown had one of Henry Ford's Model T motorcars either.

Now then, that leaves us with just one Swope family member left to meet; Poncho, the dog. As you know, no good story is complete without the inclusion of a faithful dog, and this one is no exception. Poncho was a Great Pyrenees, and if you don't know anything about Great Pyreneeses, then I should tell you that they are very large, so large in fact that Poncho could place his paws on the children's shoulders to hug them when they returned home from school. His fur coat was snowy white, and he was so very fluffy that he was wonderfully comfy to lie against in the evenings by the fire. The only member of the family who did not adore Poncho was baby Isabelle, for when she was left unattended, Poncho sometimes snatched her food or slobbered all over her face in an attempt to bathe her.

Did I mention the year was 1920? Heavens, I hope so! And you'll do well to remember this, because the story would seem awfully strange if you believed it to have taken place in the year two-thousand-something-or-another. The thing about 1920 though (and this may sadden my more youthful readers), is that there were no televisions, mobile phones, video games, computers, or the like. But you'll find that the Swope children were never wanting in amusement, and if they knew of such playthings now, they'd surely scoff and banter on about the good old days when they'd been young. We might as well begin our story on just such a day, one that began in the field behind the children's house where they were often found playing in their neighbor's broken down motorcar.

"Release the break! Release the break!" Everett was heard to shout.

"I can't!" cried Charles, who had never been in the driver's seat of a motorcar before, and was not quite sure of himself. Previously, Everett had deemed Charles too young to operate a stationary vehicle, and had only just today informed him that he had finally "come of age".

Everett growled rather menacingly at his younger sibling. "It's not that you can't, it's that you don't *dare* to!"

Charles yanked on the break shaft until both his hands were very sore, but nothing the least bit exciting happened.

"Blimey," Everett sighed, feeling as though their day of pretend driving was not off to a very good start. "Hand it over, mate!" he said authoritatively.

Charles quickly slid over into the passenger seat. He was seldom disagreeable when it came to his elder brother's orders, and truth be told, he had found the duty of driving a motorcar quite arduous, and was rather relieved to be free of it.

Everett cranked the brake, which seemed to be the trick of the thing, and then twisted the cap atop his head round so that he should look the proper motorist. He then made engine noises in the back of his throat, and instructed Charles to do the same so that the experience would be all the more convincing.

With the car purring happily beneath the hood, Everett began spinning the steering-wheel from side to side with his nose held firmly in the air, in the way their father was wont to do on their Sunday drives to church.

"Where to, Charlie?" shouted Everett. He'd often noticed that people were prone to shouting when riding in motorcars, and he rather thought it was due to the wind. Though it's true a vehicle only pretending to drive experiences very little wind, Everett saw no need to tamper with a sound system.

"I have some business in Hampshire to attend to," said Charles, who was quite good at imaginary games.

"Ahh, Hampshire is wonderful this time of year!" Everett exclaimed, and he held onto his hat as they hit a particularly strong patch of wind.

Charles and Everett found the pretend roads very bumpy indeed, and so there was quite a lot of bouncing up and down upon the red-leather seats. In a display of theatrics, Everett skillfully avoided pot holes and the occasional furry animal, and when the need arose, he squeezed the horn at allegedly incompetent motorists.

"It's quite a beautiful day! Is it not, my good man?" commented Charles, pretending to be a portly Barrister or a wealthy Duke surveying a shining spans of English countryside through the windshield. Being a passenger, thought Charles, was quite a lot more thrilling!

"It is indeed a lovely day, your Lordship! So lovely that I don't see why we shouldn't pull back the cover and let some sunlight in?" suggested Everett, feeling around the edge of the cloth roof for whatever mechanism held it in place.

"Everett, we mustn't!" pleaded Charles, slipping out of character. "He'll be awfully cross with us if we damage it." Charles of course was referring to the owner of the car who lived across the field. Though Everett and Charles had been introduced to the gentleman in question on more than one occasion, his name was something or another they never could manage to pronounce, and so instead they referred to him as The Man with the Very Large Mustache Indeed, which was a lengthy name, but one they could remember nonetheless.

"Oh come off it!" snapped Everett. "It's not like I was planning to rip it to pieces." He placed his hands back on the steering wheel, and continued to make engine purring noises in the back of his throat.

"All the same, I think it best if we didn't touch it," said Charles firmly. "Now, take a right up at the next intersection. And step on it — I'm late for an engagement."

"Right!" replied Everett, rising to the challenge with a mighty engine growl.

They played like this for several more hours, only stopping when they heard their mother's voice trailing out the kitchen window to announce dinner.

"Lucky we made it back in time, wasn't it?" said Charles, waiting for Everett to come round the passenger side and open the door for him.

"T'isn't lucky at all!" said Everett, removing his hat and giving a bow as Charles stepped from the car. "Merely a testament to my expert driving ability."

Charles felt inside his overcoat for a make-believe wallet and then handed Everett several invisible bills. "For your service, my lad," he said with an important cough. "Keep the change."

The dutiful driver tipped his hat in appreciation. "You're too kind. Though you won't mind if I check to make sure it isn't counterfeit, will you?" said Everett, holding each of the bills up to the fading sunlight. "Got swindled on my last job, you know."

"Oh yes, quite understandable. Always best to check. Those things *will* happen," bantered Charles, still pretending to have a thick stomach, several chins, and a royal title.

Once it was certain the bills were indeed legitimate, Everett patted the hood of the car and he and Charles then made their way home through the field toward their house.

"Maybe tomorrow the car will actually start," said Everett hopefully. He did say this from time to time, and then was always slightly disappointed the next day when yanking on the hand crank yielded no better results.

"But The Man with the Very Large Mustache Indeed said it won't start ... hasn't for ages," Charles reminded him, as he frequently did on these occasions, for Charles was the less adventuresome of the two and was quite sure that he preferred pretend-driving to the actual thing.

In truth, Charles preferred pretending most things over doing them, which is probably why he thought he might like to be a writer when he grew up. He prided himself on having once read two-thirds of *Oliver Twist*, which was quite remarkable for a boy of seven, he thought.

Everett, on the other hand, had no idea what he wanted to do when he grew up, but he hoped it would be something to do with cars. Everett loved cars, and loved scraping his knees and getting into things he probably oughtn't to be getting into, and he never felt he'd accomplished anything unless he came home with a pair of dirty short pants. If it had been *their* broken down motorcar out in the field, he'd have surely stolen a peek under the hood in hopes that something might look amiss and he'd be able to fix it.

The gentleman with the mustache had in fact told the children exactly what was ailing the poor motorcar once, but he had described the trouble using so many words they had never heard before and which they never cared to hear again, that they decided they really needn't know exactly why the car wouldn't start after all. And from that day on, they simply pretended that it did, which was just as well, seeing as neither one of them was old enough to be licensed anyhow.

They arrived home for dinner that evening to find cold roast beef and boiled potatoes on the table. There were also peas, which Charles liked but Everett usually hid beneath his leftover potatoes. Other times he'd flick them at baby Isabelle in her high-chair when no one was looking, and she'd snatch them up and eat them without ever considering how awful they tasted.

Their mother was in the middle of pouring them each a glass of water. "Hello, darlings," she said, smiling at them. (Mrs. Swope really was a dear). "Go wash up for dinner. Your father will be in from the store any minute now."

Charles and Everett did as they were told and squeezed one after the other into the wash closet to clean their hands. They still felt it rather strange having a bathroom on the *inside* of the house. Charles in particular wondered if they might not all drown in their sleep one night should a spigot forget to turn off, or the toilet overexcite itself. But it was quite a luxury to have running water in 1920, and the Swopes's house was one of only a handful of homes north of the city that did.

When they'd lived in England, they had gotten water from a well, done their washing in a creek, and paid calls of nature in the old outhouse out back — the latter being one rather smelly part of their lives in England that Everett and Charles seldom missed. Their mother had not shared these feelings, however. She'd felt so sentimental about the outhouse that she'd cried when it had gotten very old and rotted and needed taking down. Often prone to poetry writing in moments of intense emotion, she had composed a poem for the occasion, and even in their new home it hung proudly on the wall beside the bathroom door. It read:

> Down by the old back house
> in use so many years
> today their knocking down our treasure
> as we stand by in tears.
> The door was always open
> to each and everyone
> now all we have left of our treasure
> are the ashes beneath the sun.

Charles and Everett returned from the bathroom to find their father already seated at the head of the table, and Poncho in place at his feet waiting to collect any scraps of food that may have otherwise gone to waste upon the kitchen floor. Poncho had a bad habit of begging, and it didn't help that his head was the perfect height to rest upon the edge of the table. Charles and Everett had tried to teach Poncho proper manners one summer, but it turned out Poncho wasn't one for learning. Dogs do have very little brains after all.

"Hello, Father," said both boys together, taking their seats. "Guess where we've been today?" said Charles this time.

Their father squinted his great forehead in thought. "I must say, I'm stumped," he said.

"We've been to Hampshire in the motorcar," said Everett.

"On business," said Charles.

"Have you really? How nice. Hampshire is wonderful this time of year," said Father, kindly.

Charles clapped his hands together. "That's just what Everett said!"

Mother joined them at the table after placing baby Isabelle in her high chair, and they began to eat. Everett and Charles had to try very hard not to speak with their mouths full of beef and potatoes, which is a difficult thing to remember when you're eight and seven years old.

"Did you boys finish up your lessons?" asked their mother. "It's no good playing when you have things such as lessons hanging over your head."

"Yes, Mother," said Everett once he'd properly swallowed.

"All except the arithmetic," said Charles sheepishly, not being one for figures.

Mother smiled. Charles did not like for people to know that he counted on his fingers, but Mother never made him feel sorry for this. "We'll work on it together before you go out to play tomorrow."

The next day would be Saturday, and Charles and Everett were happy not to have school, though on the whole they did not mind school as some of the other children did. A teacher had once told them that if children refused to learn their brains would rot, which they thought sounded altogether unpleasant.

Father, who'd been salting his potatoes while Mother wasn't looking, then said, "Had we any mail today, dear?"

"Yes, a whole trunk full," she replied.

To this, Father raised his eyebrows. "A trunk, darling?"

"Mm hmm," she sang. "From the Baron ... your uncle, you know."

"Yes, yes, of course," said Father. "I wonder what it could be. Poor fellow's been dead nearly three months now." Father pushed his peas around his plate while he thought. Everett meanwhile discretely tipped a forkful of his own peas onto the floor for Poncho.

"I suspect it's your inheritance," Mother suggested.

"Huh. Didn't know the old man thought so well of me," he said. "Where is this trunk anyhow?"

Mother pointed to the fireplace where a large wooden trunk with deep groves and a golden latch sat before the hearth.

Both boys turned in their chairs to have a look. "Oooh, how exciting!" cried Charles. "Trunks are always full of magical things in books."

"May we open it with you after supper, Father?" asked Everett boldly, though he wondered if it was quite polite to help other people open their inheritances.

"Course you may," said Father.

With that settled, they finished their dinners, all except baby Isabelle who preferred her mashed carrots on her bib rather than in her mouth, and Mother sweetly offered to wash the dishes so that they could get on with the business of the trunk.

"Do hurry back," cried Charles as Father left to fetch a hammer from the tool shed. "I shouldn't like to think of something alive in there that's been waiting for hours to breathe."

"Oh, don't be stupid," said Everett crossly. "People don't send living things in trunks through the mail without poking holes in the top first."

Charles found himself with rather hurt feelings, and might have had a good sulk if Father hadn't returned and begun to pry the lid of the trunk open with the pointy end of a hammer.

"Almost there!" said Everett eagerly as Father pried up the last corner.

"Now, boys," said Father with his hands poised over the lid ready to lift it off the trunk. "I should warn you ... your great-uncle, the Baron, was awfully mischievous. If anything should leap out at me or spit poisonous venom, you both are to save yourselves and run as far away as possible. Understood?"

Both boys tried not to appear alarmed, though Charles perhaps went a bit pale. "But Everett said there couldn't be anything living inside the trunk because there aren't any holes poked in the top!" he said.

Father's eyes twinkled in the light of the fire. "Well, I'm sorry, but that's just not so. Magical creatures need very little air in comparison to other living things, you know."

Charles glared at Everett and gave a distinctive *humph*. Everett, however, pretended not to notice.

"We promise, Father. Do be brave," said Everett, and they all held their breath as the lid was lifted off the trunk.

At first no one spoke. There was so much to look at that none of them knew exactly what to comment upon first. There was a ruby red cloak, a rather worn top hat, a pair of handcuffs, several loose feathers (which worried Charles considering Father's magical creature comment), an empty bird cage, a deck of musty tarot cards, and a stuffed squirrel. There were probably lots more things buried farther down, but these would take some time to get to.

Father grabbed the top hat and chuckled as he placed it upon his head. "Your great-uncle, may he rest in peace, was always one for theatrics. Used to put on magic shows for all us kids when I was very little," he told them.

"What sort of magic shows?" asked Charles, trying not to stare at the stuffed squirrel, for its eyes were uncomfortably lifelike.

"Oh, nothing like you've ever seen before, surely," said Father. "He could make the most unimaginable things happen. Things no ordinary street magician would ever dream of. He could speak any language we ever asked him to, and play all sorts of musical instruments. He could talk to animals, and predict the future ..." Father seemed to be recalling all his favorites.

"Did he ever predict your future, Father?" asked Everett.

"Oh, yes, of course," he said. "But a person's future is very personal, and it must not be shared with anyone other than the person it pertains to."

Neither Everett nor Charles liked this rule very much. "Couldn't you tell us even just a *little* of what your uncle predicted?" asked Everett.

Father sighed. "Well, I suppose I could tell you the bit that's already come true," he said seriously, "but that's all". He drew in a deep breath. "Now let's see ... Uncle said that I would marry the loveliest lady in all of England, which was very true indeed, and that I would have three children of varying levels of difficulty."

Mother, who was now seated by the fire, smiled. She was mending a pair of socks in her lap while baby Isabelle crawled around the floor wondering what the various objects from the trunk must taste like. She'd just placed a feather part way into her mouth when Poncho decided he'd quite like to taste the feather too, which made for a rather slobbery situation for baby Isabelle. She was very pouty from then on, and Mother took her into her lap and hummed quietly so as to cheer her up.

"'Varying levels of difficulty'?" Everett repeated coldly. "He must mean you, Charles. You're the difficultest, certainly."

Charles, who always tried his hardest to mind his manners and behave properly, wasn't about to stand for such an injustice. "You're a beast, Everett. And 'difficultest' isn't even a word." (This is where lesser children may have stuck out their tongue).

Father did not give Everett a chance to defend his poor grammar. "We'll have none of your quarreling now, please. There's loads more in this trunk to dig through," he said, not unkindly, and continued to sort through his inheritance.

Now, when you become eight and seven years of age, you might find as Everett and Charles did that pride is a very tricky thing, and if you've already past eight and seven years of age, then I probably don't have to tell you this. But despite their sometimes tricky pride, Everett and Charles decided to set aside their ill tempers for the good of this evening with their father, for it wasn't all fathers who were willing to sit upon the floor and dig through old trunks with their children. In fact, many fathers often feel themselves much too big or too busy to play on the floor, or to play anywhere for that matter, and for this reason the Swope children were very grateful that Mr. Swope wasn't one of those fathers.

Everett and Charles helped to dig and dig and dig, unearthing another pair of handcuffs, a quill pen, an old oil lamp, two large seashells, a harmonica, and ...

Each of them blinked. At the bottom of the trunk, somehow unharmed by the mounds of trinkets once piled upon it, was a periwinkle blue turban. Though I shall tell you now that the turban was most conclusively periwinkle blue, this fact would be much disputed between the children in times to come. But for the benefit of your imagination, I will not delay the truth, and I must ask you not to doubt the perwinkleness of the turban from this point forth.

Father's face lit up and he reached for the turban, removing it from a wire shaped head the likes of which very old gentlemen use to display their toupees when not in use. "This," he said, holding the turban up in the air, "is what your great-uncle always wore when performing magic."

Charles reached up to touch it. "Does it have magical powers, you think?" he asked.

"Oh, I suspect so," Father replied. "Uncle always said that it did."

"Then we should probably test it out on the dog," said Everett decidedly, and at this suggestion, Poncho sniffed around the silk creases of the turban in curiosity.

Father agreed that this was surely the best thing to do, and he plopped the turban snugly down atop Poncho's head. They waited anxiously for the dog to glow green or cough up fairy dust, but nothing interesting like this came about. Nevertheless, it couldn't be denied how very smart the dog looked.

"I think he likes it," said Charles. Poncho, however, may have begged to differ had he been the talking sort of dog.

"Maybe so," said Father, "but we mustn't wear out its magic all at once. Magic, you see, is a finicky thing." This was rather a wise thing to say, the children thought, and they watched as Father lifted the turban off Poncho's head and placed it carefully back into the trunk ...

Like Charles and Everett, you might be feeling very curious about the turban just now, and you probably should be for I went to great lengths to mention it in the title of this book. However, I'm afraid that's the last you'll hear of it in this chapter because the children's bedtime fell quite inconveniently at this point in our story. Things are what they are, do not blame me.

It was upon the stroke of eight o'clock that Everett and Charles heard the words which all eight and seven year olds who possess even an ounce of dignity dread to hear. You know the ones ... their mother said them as she stoked the remaining embers of the fire. "I think it's up to bed for you two," was how she put it, I believe, and if you've ever had a bedtime, I'm sure you know just how saddening these sort of words can be.

Everett, feeling bound by honor to protest at least a little, said "Oh, must we really, Mother?" despite his not being entirely disagreeable to the idea of crawling under the warm covers. "Things have only just gotten exciting."

"Come now," said their father this time, "the trunk will still be here in the morning."

And so, not wishing to appear especially mutinous, they went to bed, and the next morning the trunk was still there just as Father had said it would be. As for the turban, the Swope children would not give it another thought for quite some time.

In Which Father's Grocery Store Suffers A Catastrophe

You'll remember I told you that the trunk was still there the next morning, and I assure you this wasn't a lie, for as your friend I shall never lie to you, but to be quite truthful, the trunk was of very little consequence on this particular day (or for many days after) owing to some rather extraordinary events that took place.

At breakfast that morning, Everett and Charles were eating their oatmeal when Father came down the stairs whistling a happy tune, as was usual on mornings when the sun was particularly bright. He gave Mother a kiss on the cheek and poured himself a cup of black coffee, which he always said was the only way he could manage to stay awake when Old Lady Mulberry came into the store for her daily nectarine, never parting without updating Father on her poor cat's kidney troubles.

"You boys must visit me in the store this morning," said Father. "We're expecting a pumpkin delivery ... picked them out myself yesterday up at Mr. Cooper's farm — ones as big as Poncho!" he boasted. The dog perked up eagerly at the sound of his name, but one look from Father and he laid his head back down on the floor with a heavy sigh.

"May we have a pumpkin for Halloween this year, Father?" asked Everett. "I should like to carve The Man With The Very Large Mustache Indeed."

"And why is that?" asked Mother, who was tying a bonnet around baby Isabelle's head.

"I've always wondered what a pumpkin would look like with a mustache," replied Everett, and Charles nodded in agreement.

Father choked on his coffee. "Well, I don't see why we shouldn't have a pumpkin," he said once his breathing had been restored. "I'll help you pick one out."

"—*Only* after you've finished your arithmetic, Charles," Mother amended, when she saw that both boys had begun to eat much more quickly in excitement for visiting the store. Their spoons shoveled into their mouths a little less hastily from then on.

It took Charles well over an hour to master his times tables up through the number ten, and if Mother hadn't made him sit on his hands, he'd have ended up with awfully sore fingers. Meanwhile, Everett had played on the floor with his toy fire engine, resisting the urge to call out answers or brag about how quickly he'd learned his

20

own times tables. *"Thou shall not boast,"* he reminded himself, recalling the ten commandments, though once he'd thought this he began to wonder if he'd gotten it quite right.

"Run along now, my darlings," said Mother, "but be sure not to disrupt Father while he's with a customer."

Everett and Charles promised they wouldn't, and entered the store through the rear door, which was also the front door of the house, if you could consider front doors the same things as rear doors. At the back of the grocery store was a little stockroom full of cartons and crates, and several ice boxes, and the children had to be sure to tread carefully so as not to stub their toes or bang their knees.

"Watch yer'selves! I'm a comin' through," said a low voice on this occasion, though at first all Charles and Everett saw was a pair of legs and several stacked boxes of lettuce heading toward them. They soon spotted the dark face of Watson, Father's produce man, struggling to peer over the top of the lettuce on his way into the store.

"Mind you, I wouldn't argue if one of ya's offered to get the door," the man added sardonically.

"Of course!" said Everett, lunging forward to hold open the swinging door, though he thought Watson might have at least said "hello" to them.

The man thanked them, and as if reading Everett's mind, he said, "—oh, and hello by the way."

"Good morning!" cried the children, brightly.

Charles and Everett were quite used to Watson's presence by now, for he'd taken the job with Father soon after the store's opening, and had rented the little room above the children's nursery ever since. Sometimes on chilly evenings, they'd ask him downstairs to sit with them by the fire, and he'd chat happily with Mother or talk business with Father. He'd come to feel quite like family to the Swopes, and at Mother's insistence, had even joined them for the past few holiday suppers.

The thing Charles and Everett liked best about Watson was that he never talked to them as though they were little boys, for even the most childlike of children hate this rather annoying habit of many adults. This was perhaps because Watson knew better than some people what it was like being made to feel small and inferior. You see, Watson was black, which is quite as nice a thing to be as being white, but in 1920 there were rather a lot of people who did not think so. In fact, they were often times unfriendly and unfair to black people, something which angered Mr. Swope to no end.

The boys followed Watson in through the store and traveled down the dairy aisle toward the cash register where their father was busy ringing up Mrs. Mulberry's nectarine.

"—three drops a day, the vet says, and Harriet's been ever so brave – she never puts up a fuss – drops her little mouth right open for me to apply the medication," she was telling Father in a steady stream of sentences that hardly knew where they were beginning, or when they should end. "—does make her awfully sleepy though, but the important thing is she's feeling much better, bless the—"

"How nice, Mrs. Mulberry. I'm so pleased for you," interjected Father upon spotting Charles and Everett.

"You will excuse me, I hope — my sons are here and I'm sure they must have something very important to tell me. Give my love to Harriet!"

"Oh, yes, that's very kind. She'll like that," replied the old woman, taking hold of the bagged nectarine Father'd been holding out in front of her. She appraised Charles and Everett with a wrinkled smile as though checking to see that they indeed appeared to be in possession of some important information.

"Good-day, Mrs. Mulberry," said both Charles and Everett nicely.

"Eh-hem, yes, well ... Good-day to you, children," she said with a nod in Father's direction. She then ambled out of the store grinning as only someone who spent her days with a cat and a nectarine could grin.

Everett and Charles felt slightly uncomfortable with their father now peering down at them over the countertop. "We don't *really* have anything to tell you, Father," said Everett.

"We've come about the pumpkins," added Charles.

"Well, of course you have," said Father, coming round to greet them. "I only said that to get rid of poor old Mrs. Mulberry. A chap can only take so much talk of cats and medications, you know."

The children *did* know this, for they sometimes ran into Mrs. Mulberry in the park walking Harriet the cat on a little lead, and they were often detained for several minutes, forced to pet the cat and endure its scratching at their shoes while its owner boasted endlessly about it. Charles and Everett usually wished they could run in the opposite direction when they saw her coming, but Mother suspected she was rather lonely and said the children were doing a good deed by talking to her. Charles had then conceded that if he were very old and lonely, he might like to have two kind little children such as themselves to talk to as well.

"Anyway, the delivery truck should be here any moment," Father told them, peering out the store window in which many canned goods and jams were on display. "Ah yes — here it comes now, I think."

Everett and Charles pressed their noses to the glass to take a peek at the mud-covered pick-up truck as it backed up to the store. Father was about to open the door, but just then a gentleman wondering about cheeses begged for his attention.

"Yes, well — be right with you, sir," said Father. "Watson! — attend to the pumpkins for me, will you? — and children, you stay out of the way now." And with that he trotted off to help the cheese curious customer, and Watson dutifully stepped out the door, leaving it wide open for the delivery.

"Oh no!" gasped Everett as a large bearded man hopped from the truck and put out a cigarette under his boot. "It's Mean Old Barney Lucas," he whispered to Charles.

"You mean—"

"Billy Lucas's father," Everett answered.

Though Charles had never met the man, he could quite see the predicament. The one and only time his brother Everett had ever thrown a punch was when Billy Lucas had called a black boy in town a really, really nasty name. I shan't tell you what it was, and I hope you never have to hear it in the whole of your life!

The boys had no time to think about disappearing back into the house before the sound of yelling outside distracted them.

"——Keep yer filthy hands off my truck," they heard Mean Old Barney Lucas growl, spitting out the side of his mouth and nearing closer and closer to Watson.

"Father, come quick!" yelled Everett, though the commotion must have reached Father's ears, for he was already leaping toward the front of the store, followed closely by his customer who was now carrying a wedge of brie.

"Back into the house, you two. *Scram!*" he yelled to them as he stumbled out the doorway. However, the boys were too frozen to move, and instead crouched under the window peering out between the jars of jam.

"What's the problem here?" said Father, with quite a lot more authority than he ever used around the house.

Barney Lucas wiped sweat from under his cap with a grubby looking handkerchief. "I ain't deliverin' Mr. Cooper's pumpkins to no black man, and I'm sure as hell not lettin' him anywhere near my truck," he spat.

Father looked incensed, but refrained from shouting. "This man works for me, and I asked him to take care of the delivery while I was with a customer."

"You mean to tell me, Swope, that this *ape* here's a paid employee of yours?" sneered Mr. Lucas, with a right ugly look upon his face. Watson in the meantime stood quietly behind Father with his hands behind his back.

"Yes," exclaimed Father, with his nose held firmly in the air, "and the only thing ape-ish around here is your behavior. Now, please make your delivery and be gone."

Everett and Charles were terribly proud of Father's bravery, but Mean Old Barney Lucas was looking meaner by the minute, and they were so worried for Father's safety that their hearts were pounding in their ears and their fingernails were digging into the windowsill.

"No can do," grunted Mr. Lucas. "I ain't makin' any deliveries here today." And he grabbed for the handle of the driver door.

Before anyone could stop him, Watson had stepped forward. "But Mr. Swope paid for those pumpkins with his hard earned money!"

Barney Lucas whipped around with his teeth bared and fists in the air. "Bloody cheek!" he seethed, leaping toward Watson.

"*No!*" Charles and Everett screamed, knocking over dozens of jam jars as they launched themselves at the window.

Father shoved Watson out of the way and ducked as Barney Lucas's fist swung through the air, clipping the top of Father's head just before pounding into the brick exterior of the grocery store with a sickening crunch.

"*Arrrrrgh!*" he shrieked in anguish, clutching at his broken fist and swearing terribly.

By this point, both Father and the gentleman with the brie were standing protectively in front of Watson.

"I want you off my property, Barney!" Father stammered, trying to catch his breath.

Mr. Lucas staggered back to his truck, yanked the door open, and thrust himself up into the driver's seat, slamming the door behind him with a pathetic whimper. He stuck his greasy head out the window, leering at Father and breathing through clenched teeth. "You'll pay for this, Swope!"

The truck roared to life, but before he pulled away, Barney pointed a stubby finger straight at Watson. "This ain't over," he added, his lip curled up in a painful grimace. The tires then spun out from underneath the truck, spraying dirt and gravel in its wake as it sped off down the country road.

As hell-bent as Mean Old Barney Lucas had been that Father wasn't to have the pumpkins, he forgot one crucial thing — to close the tailgate. So, naturally, several bolder-sized pumpkins came tumbling out the back of the truck and landed in front of the store, only one of them managing to smash itself in the process.

"I'm so sorry, Mr. Swope," pleaded Watson, following Father back into the store. "I'll pay yeh back fer those pumpkins, be it the last thing I do."

"I've told you a million times, Watson — it's Edward," said Father, wearily. (That's it! I knew Father had a name). "And you can not be held responsible for other people's prejudice. I'll have a word with Mr. Cooper — I'm sure he's not of the same mind as Barney Lucas, and if he is, then we won't be wanting his pumpkins anyway now, will we," he said.

Watson knew not to answer this, for it was by no means a question, and just then Charles and Everett slammed into his side, hugging him fiercely. He hugged each of them back, but was looking embarrassed.

"Dear Watson!" cried Charles. "We're so pleased you're safe. We were dreadfully worried!"

Father frowned slightly at the sight of them. "I thought I told you boys to go back into the house," he said.

"We were going to Father, really we were," said Charles earnestly, "but we were so frozen with fright."

"Not me — I wasn't frozen with fright," argued Everett, though we all know he was. "I stayed in case you needed protecting," he said.

"Little boys shouldn't go protecting people from men the size of Barney Lucas," said Father sternly. "They'll find themselves with many broken bones."

Everett felt a bit wounded by the "little boys" comment, but was so happy Father and Watson were okay that he soon forgot his pride. He and Charles then helped Father to relay the story of the pumpkin scuffle to Mother over supper, both of them jumping in to provide the more dramatic bits which Father seemed quick to pass over.

Mother was very worried indeed, and her worrying led to quite a lot more worrying on Charles and Everett's part as well.

"Surely there's no need for all this upset," said Father, always the voice of reason.

"Of course there isn't," Mother agreed, trying her best to sound cheerful. "Why, many people love Watson and will want to look out for him. Mr. Lucas is a *bad* man, that's all, but for every bad man there's a hundred good ones just looking for people to be nice too."

This was rather a pleasant thought, but Charles and Everett didn't seem able to wipe the worried looks from their faces as they stared pensively into their bowls of soup. Mean Old Barney Lucas had been horribly angry about his broken hand, and they thought he looked as though he'd quite like to break something of Father's or Watson's as well.

Mother sighed and flung her napkin down upon the table. "Oh, don't let's be gloomy!" she said. "Let's talk about something else, shall we? Everett, would you still like to be a pirate for Halloween? These matters must be considered — Halloween is only a few days away, you know, and I'll be needing to order the fabric."

And so a nice discussion of Halloween festivities ensued, and everyone was soon feeling jolly again. Charles had decided to be an Egyptian because he'd just read the most thrilling book about an Egyptian and an amulet, and Mother had said she could lend him a very amulet-looking necklace if he liked, so long as he promised not to bury it or sell it to a pirate.

Thoughts of a worrisome nature subsided in the days leading up to Halloween, and there were no further sightings of Barney Lucas. Charles and Everett attended school, while at home Mother was fast at work on their costumes, including one for Poncho, whom they'd decided would be going as a policeman, for they already had the handcuffs.

In the evenings, the children attempted to carve The Man With The Very Large Mustache Indeed into the pumpkins Father and Watson had drug in from out front of the store, but in the end it had been Watson who'd carved the most convincing mustache. He'd kindly offered to let the children tell their friends that *they* had been the ones to carve the mustached pumpkin, but after the initial excitement of this thought, Charles and Everett wondered if this wouldn't be quite like lying, and decided instead to tell their friends what a clever produce man their Father had. This pleased Mother and Father greatly, for teaching your children about the wrongness of lying can be a frightfully complicated task.

Charles and Everett were so eager for Halloween to arrive, that once it had, they quite wished it hadn't so quickly. The best things always seem to happen much too fast, don't they? I've never understood why this should be the case when nasty things such as dentist visits and school exams insist upon dragging themselves out to such unbearable proportions, but there you have it.

After supper on the evening of All Hallows' Eve, Mother was fitting Charles and Everett into their costumes while the boys discussed the rhymes and songs they should shout at their neighbors after banging upon their doors. This particular tradition has fallen by the wayside in recent years, but a hundred years ago it was quite customary to shout things at your neighbors on Halloween.

Charles, who was quicker with words, suggested:

Nuts and sweets I like to eat
so please don't be a mean-y,
for I'll scream and shout and stomp my feet
if candies you don't feed me.

On my face I wear a mask
so you shan't chance to see me,
but if you do all that I ask
I'll wish you happy Halloween-y!

Now you might be thinking this poem is a teensy bit rude, and to say such things to your neighbor on any other day of the year most certainly would be, but Mother knew that Halloween was all about good-natured pranks and practical jokes, and found Charles's poem very clever indeed.

She clapped her hands together when he had finished. "How splendid!" she said, for Mother loved a good poem.

Not wishing to be left out, Everett then thought very hard to compose his own poem, thinking up many fancy words, and trying to string them together as hard as ever he could, but no matter how hard he tried, the words Everett strung together seemed quite incapable of rhyming, and as you know, poems are hardly any fun at all if they don't rhyme. It's only very boring adults who enjoy dull, rhyme-less poems.

"Never you mind," Mother told Everett, sweetly. "I don't suspect pirates are often very good at poetry."

Father then entered in from the shop carrying handfuls of candles and firecrackers for the boys to use, and a bag of apples for the neighborhood children to bob for. Bobbing for apples was another Halloween tradition, though not one Charles was especially fond of. Everett, having what Father sometimes called "a very large mouth", was much better at it.

"My, aren't you a scary pirate!" said Father to Everett. "And you, sir," he said to Charles, "are a most convincing Egyptian."

"Don't forget to compliment Poncho's costume too," Mother reminded him, for Poncho was sitting very politely in his policeman's uniform beside Father, looking very white and fluffy poking out of a navy blue jacket with brass buttons, and a black helmet. Mother had even sewn him a nice little badge.

"You're the picture of authority, Poncho," Father remarked, scratching the dog behind the ears. "Now boys, you best be heading out — the sun's just gone down. Be back by ten, and remember — don't let anyone pull any pranks with Mrs. Mulberry's cat, or I'll never hear the end of it. The poor devil's on enough medication as it is."

"Got it," said Everett.

"Yes, Father," said Charles.

And with that, they finished off their costumes with a few accessories Father'd lent them from the trunk — a feather for Everett's pirate hat, a pair of handcuffs for Poncho, and the old oil lamp for Charles, which they all agreed had every possibility of containing a genie.

"Where shall we set off the fireworks?" Charles asked Everett as they stepped into the street, each carrying a lit candle. Poncho followed close behind them, the handcuffs dangling from his collar.

The wind whipped around their shoulders, and leaves blew about their feet, and the only light spilling into the street was the golden glow of jack-o'-lanterns upon neighboring porches. Altogether, this made for the start of a very spooky evening, though neither Charles nor Everett would have admitted as much.

"Best do it in the field out by the old motorcar," said Everett. "It's on a bit of a hill, so they'll be seen quite plainly. Jimmy Holbrook and Bobby Smalls are coming, and some others — they know to look for the fireworks."

Trudging up the hill, they lit a bundle of fireworks with the tip of Everett's candle, and then waited in the old motorcar for the others to arrive. The fireworks popped, crackled, and hissed, and soon the night sky was aglow with sprays of red sparks and great puffs of smoke.

"Here they come now," said Everett a few moments later, spotting several figures climbing the hill under the remaining flashes of light up in the sky.

"I hope it's them and not zombies," said Charles with a shiver.

"Oh, do be quiet," snapped Everett. "You say the most unintellectuable things when you're afraid."

"Un-*intelligible*," corrected Charles. "And I'm not afraid," he said, which was a lie.

Everett shrugged. "Whatever."

Then came a voice calling out a short way off. "Is that you, Swope?"

"Yep!" Everett called back. "We're up here, Smalls! Hope you left your scaredy pants at home — this night won't be for the faint-hearted," he shouted, glaring for a moment at his brother Charles, whose oil lamp was chattering.

"Don't be so sure of yourself," replied Bobby Smalls as he reached the top of the hill with Jimmy Holbrook and a few other boys Charles and Everett recognized from school. Jimmy, coincidentally, was dressed as a zombie, and was looking thoroughly disgruntled about something, likely the presence of his younger sister, Dotty, who'd insisted upon tagging along, dressed as a kitten, complete with whiskers.

"Now listen up," said Everett once they had all gathered round. "You all know what we have to do. First, we bob for apples, and then the loser must run up and bang on Grouchy Mr. Granger's front door." Grouchy Mr. Granger was the scariest man in the neighborhood, owing to the fact that Mean Old Barney Lucas technically lived one town over. Like most grouchy people however, Grouchy Mr. Granger was really quite nice, but everyone was so off-put by his grouchy exterior that nobody knew this. It probably didn't help that one of his eyes bulged, and the other one was a bright orange.

"What's the loser to do once they bang upon the door?" said a boy dressed in a white sheet with holes poked out for his eyes.

"Ah, yes, I've been thinking about that," said Everett. "I vote that the loser has to call Mr. Granger a 'nasty vampire' and then throw minced garlic in his face before running away."

Several of them nodded in agreement, for this was a brilliantly mischievous plan. "But who has minced garlic on them?" said Bobby Smalls.

"Well, *I do*, of course," said Everett. "It was my idea." And he patted a leather pelt around his waist in which he'd placed the garlic. "So that's settled then. Now — before we set out upon the completion of this dangerous task, is there any man amongst us ill-equipped to summon the necessary bravery?"

All eyes turned to Dotty. "Well, I suppose I'm not a man at all," she said meekly, holding onto her tail. "But I do so wish to be one, just for tonight. Oh please, *please* — let me come with you!"

"Hmm, well," considered Everett. "We shall have to hold a committee," he said. (Everett did have a wicked streak when left in charge.) "Huddle!" he cried, and all the boys gathered near. There was then quite a lot of grumbling and nodding of heads, and a fair bit of finger pointing as well. Finally, the huddle dispersed and Everett said, "Fine. You may stay."

"Oh, thank you!" the kitten cried. "It's ever so kind of you — I promise I won't be a bother, and I'll be very brave—"

"That's the trouble with girls, you see," said Everett to Charles, quite ignoring Dotty's speech, "—they do go on so." This was a very unfair statement to make though, for boys can go on too, and often about the most mundane things like the inner workings of cars or rugby strategies, but you never will convince boys of this.

The troop of masked children and Poncho then trudged back down the hill toward the Swope house, where Mr. Swope had left them a large trough of water and some apples. Once they'd each flexed their jaws in preparation, Everett cried "On your marks, men! (and lady). Get ready — set —" but instead of shouting "Go!" Everett launched his face at the nearest apple, and the other boys (and girl) quickly followed suit.

Water splashed from all sides as six or seven faces bobbed over and over again into the trough, plucking as many apples as possible from the surface. Then, after several jaw-agonizing minutes, Dotty Holbrook's teeth sank into the last remaining apple, and Everett, now quite drenched, shouted "Time's up!"

Dotty was looking pleased with herself, for she'd faired quite nicely, and had five apples sitting on the grass beside her. Everett was looking even more pleased with himself, as his pile must have contained at least eight or nine apples. All said and done, each of the boys had fetched three or more apples — that is, all except for Charles.

"Oh, bother," said Everett, realizing that his own brother had lost.

Charles, whom as I said never liked bobbing for apples, looked close to tears, and if it hadn't been for fear of causing his brother further embarrassment, he might have had a good cry.

"Well, you know what this means," said Bobby.

"Right," said Everett, unhooking the leather strap and holding the garlic out in front of him.

Cowering, Charles reached out for the pelt and slowly placed it around his own waist. "Can't someone else be brave?" he said. "I shake so, you see — when being brave — and I shouldn't like to upset the pelt and sling garlic all over the ground."

"You shan't upset the pelt," barked Everett. "I forbid you from upsetting the pelt. And you don't shake for being brave, you shake for being scared, I tell you. Now, be gone! We'll wait for you out by Grouchy Mr. Granger's mailbox till you've finished the deed."

Several boys gave Charles a supportive pat on the back before trotting off down the street toward the aforesaid Grouchy Mr. Granger's house, though Dotty stayed behind for a moment.

"I'll go with you and hold your hand if you like," she said, kindly. "Nothing's so bad when you have a friend."

"No," said Charles quite coldly, still with hurt feelings, but he soon added "Thank you", remembering his manners. After all, she was only trying to be nice, which was more than he could say for Everett at the moment. Older brothers do have their nasty ways, don't they?

Charles and Dotty followed behind the pack of other boys, though perhaps a little less eagerly. Charles had thought about asking if he might take Poncho with him to go bang upon Mr. Granger's door, but the dog looked quite in league with Everett, Bobby, Jimmy, and the others, running happily alongside them. Charles would just have to face the mean old man all alone, for he definitely wasn't taking a girl along with him. (Even Charles had his prejudices.)

A great, steep hill lined with evergreens loomed ahead of them, and an old wooden house with many gables and crooked shutters sat atop it, illuminated only by a solitary porch light.

"Welp, here we are!" said Everett, slightly out of breath and leaning upon a lopsided mailbox. "Good luck then!"

Several of the others wished Charles good luck as well, for it's very easy to wish others luck when you're not the one needing it, but he then thought he heard Bobby whisper something that sounded like *"He's a goner"* to Jimmy, and Charles felt his insides give a little tumble.

"I must be brave, I must be brave," Charles chanted under his breath as he began his ascent up the hill, occasionally glancing over his shoulder for moral support, which consisted merely of Everett making shooing motions with his hands, and Dotty waving energetically to him with her paw.

The night air seemed to grow chillier and chillier the higher and higher Charles crept. "Maybe no one will be home," he consoled himself as he grew nearer to the door, ever so painstakingly.

At last, Charles stepped up onto the porch and drew a deep breath, which filled his lungs with a tremendous shudder.

"Go on!" someone shouted down below when it seemed as though Charles may idle on the doorstep indefinitely.

He took another step forward, cringing at the sight of cobwebs, and at the sound of the wind as it whistled its way in and out through cracks in the door. Mustering up every last ounce of courage, Charles knew what he must do. With icy cold fingers, he scooped a handful of minced garlic from inside the pelt and knocked thrice upon the door.

The air seemed to grow chillier yet and the porch light dimmer as Charles stood shaking on the spot, only breathing once or twice while he prayed for the door to remain unanswered. The children below began to grumble in restless disappointment, and Charles was soon wondering if his prayers mightn't have been answered when suddenly there came the tell-tale clicking noise of a lock being unlatched and a chain being drawn, and the great oak door then swung open in an ear piercing chorus of groans and creaks.

A ghastly grouchy looking man with bulgy eyes and sallow skin towered in the doorway, scowling at the quivering figure on his doorstep. Charles's heart leapt through his chest, and with no time left to think, he did what he knew he must do — he flung the fistful of garlic straight at Grouchy Mr. Granger's face.

The man sputtered indignantly and flailed his arms about as if he were being attacked by a swarm of bees.

"Y-y-you're a nasty v-v-vampire, Mr. G-Granger," Charles stuttered, and then without a stitch of courage left in his body, he turned to run.

"Hold it right there!" growled the assaulted gentleman, grabbing Charles by the collar (a lovely Egyptian collar, by the way, which Mother had fastened for him).

"Oh *please*, Mr. Granger!" begged Charles, quite unable to move. "*Do* let me go! I promise I didn't mean any harm — don't be cross, *please* don't be cross — we were bobbing for apples, you see, and——"

"I say, my boy, do *be quiet!*" the man shouted, yanking Charles inside.

Everett, Bobby, Jimmy, Dotty, and the other neighborhood children all gasped, and Dotty even began to cry. "We've killed him!" one of them was heard to shout.

But inside, Charles had been put down on the entryway carpet and was now staring up to find Grouchy Mr. Granger smiling down at him. And it wasn't the sort of smile grouchy people use when they're quite happy to have caught children in the act of misbehaving, it was a delighted sort of smile — one that's usually seen upon the opening of a pleasant greeting card or beautifully wrapped package.

"Now, I know you've been put up to this," said Mr. Granger, still smiling. "Say it — you have, haven't you?"

Charles gulped. "Well, I suppose I've *sort of* been put up to it," he said. "I know it was wrong of me though, truly I do. You mustn't blame the others, I could have said no — it's just my brother, you see — he says I haven't got any honor."

Grouchy Mr. Granger beamed at him, and Charles thought he didn't look very grouchy after all. "I was young once too, you know," he said. "I know all about defending one's honor. *Listen* — seeing as it's Halloween, how about I pretend to toss you back out on the porch? I promise to put up a terrible fuss, and then you can run off and tell your friends how you managed to escape certain death."

Charles couldn't believe his luck. "*Gee,* that's awfully jolly of you, Mr. Granger!"

"Please — call me Timothy," said the man. "Only not to your friends, or they shall wonder how we've become so chummy."

"Won't it be like lying though?" asked Charles, "— pretending you're awful and all ..."

"Oh, I shouldn't think so," replied the gentleman. "It'd be wrong to spoil everyone's fun. Plus, if people knew I wasn't grouchy — yes, I know that's what they call me — there'd be folks up here all the time, and I quite like my privacy."

"You can count on me! I shan't tell anyone," said Charles.

"Thank you," said Timothy. "There's a good lad. Now, remember to run as though your life depends upon it — and it probably wouldn't hurt to scream a little too."

"Yes sir, thank you," said Charles, and wished Mr. Granger a happy Halloween before the man flung the door open and gave Charles a push that looked much more ferocious than it truly was.

"—and don't let me catch you on my property *ever* again!" he roared as Charles ran down the hill, glancing over his shoulder only once, at which point he was almost certain Mr. Granger winked at him before the door slammed shut with a terrific thud.

When Charles reached the mailbox moments later, panting for air, he was received with cheers and loud applause, and each of the children took turns patting him on the back and telling him how ripping it was that he'd been so brave. Even Poncho looked relieved to see him in one piece.

Charles was surging with pride and happiness, and took no time in providing all the horrific details.

"—thought it was the end of me," he told them. "Tried to gouge my eyes out with a scalpel, he did, but I hit him over the head with my oil lamp and ran!"

"Bloody brilliant!" cried Everett, swelling with pride.

"Oh, I just *knew* you'd be okay!" gushed Dotty.

Feeling quite lighthearted again, the children ran through the neighborhood skipping and singing and banging on people's doors to shout clever things at them and collect goodies. Charles tried his poem out on Mrs. Mulberry, who seemed quite pleased, and nobody attempted to pull any pranks on her cat.

As the evening wore on, the children's pockets became filled with candies and coins, bonfire toffees, roasted pumpkin seeds, and sweet corn. They still wished for a little more mischief though, and it was Jimmy who had the idea to play a prank on his aunt who lived just a ways up the street from the Swopes's house.

"And you're sure she won't mind?" said Bobby, once they'd planned it all out.

"Oh no! Not Aunt Mildred," Jimmy assured them. "She's a trooper, that one — loves a good laugh."

And so the children let themselves into Aunt Mildred's chicken coup and snatched each of her chickens one by one, carrying them around the front of her house (or in Poncho's case, chasing them round) and letting them loose in her screened-in porch, where they clucked in excitement and made an awful mess of the place. It was a wonderful prank, and the children were quite proud of themselves, but just as Everett and Charles were carrying round the last of the chickens, they spotted something terrible ...

I told you this would happen, as soon as I'd begun the chapter, though I had hoped maybe it wouldn't. But, I'm afraid it did. Everett was the first to spot them — figures cloaked in white with cone shaped hoods, wielding a wooden cross that'd been set on fire. There must have been a dozen of them chanting and raving as they marched down the street.

Everett grabbed Charles and hid behind some bushes, and a few of the others did the same. He'd hoped it might have only been another Halloween prank, but somehow he knew it wasn't. They watched as the cloaked figures drew near to Charles and Everett's house, and the children heard them shouting things about God, hell, damnation, and something about the "supreme race", whatever that was.

Everett hoped they would continue on their way and pass right on through town, but was horrified to see that they were instead forming a circle in front of Father's grocery store. There was nothing that Charles and Everett could have done, or that the whole troop of children could have done for that matter, but they hadn't even the chance to try before one of the hooded figures raised a fiery orb into the night sky and sent it crashing through the front window, shattering the pane of glass into a million pieces, and setting Father's grocery store alight in a blaze of flames.

In Which Cousin Clara Comes For A Visit

Now I'm sure you're quite stricken with grief, and awfully concerned about the fate of the Swopes, but seeing as this is only the third chapter, you needn't worry about our main characters leaving the story so quickly. Plus, I assure you this isn't one of those dreadfully sad stories in which the children are left orphans and sent to live with some horrible aunt in a big horrible house in a horrible faraway place without any nice people or other children to play with. Each and every Swope member survived the fire, including Poncho, and not even Watson had so much as a scratch. But Father's grocery store on the other hand ... well, it's quite gone. Not all of it, mind you, but the important bits at least.

Miraculously, the Swopes's house remained standing as firmly as ever, though it was a bit smokey smelling in the days following the fire. It had taken the Coopstown fire department till midnight to put out the blaze — way past Charles and Everett's bedtime. They'd stayed out by the street with Mother and Poncho while their father and Watson helped the firemen as best they could. Normally, Everett was quite fascinated by fire trucks, and had always wished to see a fire being put out, but this wasn't at all what he'd had in mind. Putting out fires wasn't the least bit exciting when it was your own father's grocery store in flames. And he supposed anything on fire must belong to somebody's father, mother, son or daughter, and so he made up his mind never to wish to see another fire for the rest of his life.

As for the white-hooded figures Everett and Charles had seen, it had gotten much too smokey to keep track of them after they'd set the fire, and they'd quickly disappeared. For at least a week after Halloween, both boys had dreams about the figures in the middle of the night, and when they awoke in their dark bedrooms with a shout or scream, their mother would come and comfort them, and bring them a glass of warm milk.

"Not to worry, my darlings," she'd whisper softly, and kiss their foreheads.

"But who were they, Mother?" asked Charles one evening.

Mother had seemed hesitant to speak of such things up till then. "A very bad group of people," she'd replied. "They call themselves the Ku Klux Klan, and they consider it their duty to put black people in their place."

45

Mother's cheeks flushed and she looked away. "I suspect they rather wanted to punish your father for hiring a black man and for renting him a room."

"But why should they be so mad at black people?" said Charles, which was a very good question indeed.

"I shall never understand this, dear," she'd told him. "They feel black people should be their servants, all because of the color of their skin — is that not the silliest thing you've ever heard?"

"Oh, yes," Charles had said. "Old Mrs. Mulberry has different skin — hers is very wrinkled — but nobody's asking her to be a servant."

Mother had smiled at this. "Quite right, and a very poor one she would make with her eyesight. Watson, though, is as good and honest a worker as you'll ever find, and he deserves his wages just as much as the next man. He and Father will find work soon enough — you're not to worry."

But weeks came and went, and Father and Watson hadn't found work quite so quickly. Now if you're anything like Everett and Charles, you might be wondering why Father and Watson should have to find new work at all ... why couldn't the police simply track the white-hooded figures down and demand that they pay to repair Father's store? and I quite understand you wondering this, because that would be a very fair thing to do. But, sadly, in 1920 the police were not in the habit of making the Ku Klux Klan do anything they did not feel like doing, and in all fairness, it would have been very hard to bring judgement down upon people in hoods, seeing as nobody could say for sure who was underneath them — and even if somebody could, most people would have been much too frightened to say so. Now, if a *black* person had set fire to somebody's grocery store in 1920, well that would have been an entirely different story altogether. There were many people back then who felt black people shouldn't even be able to sneeze unless they were standing in someplace specifically labeled "Black Person Sneezing Area". But the Ku Klux Klan was not to be held quite so accountable for their own actions for a good many years.

So, if you're hoping this story ends with all dozen white-hooded figures lined up in handcuffs with the Sheriff shaking his finger at them, I'm afraid you'll be sorely disappointed. I could lie to you and say this is how it happened, but as I've told you — I'm your friend, and friends should never lie to one another. However, as your friend, I *can* assure you that if you find yourself feeling persecuted by awful people who think you aren't simply wonderful just the way you are — it will get better, I promise. The Swopes loved Watson dearly and weren't about to give up on him simply because some figures in silly costumes thought they should, and there are many people who'd be willing to do the same for you. No matter how gloomy you may be feeling, I hope you never *ever* doubt this.

Now, back to the Swopes ... Without Father's grocery store, they became quite poor. I know this is awfully sudden, but I saw no reason to delay in telling you. One minute they had all the money they ever needed, and the next ... well, as I said, they were suddenly left with very limited means. Father had to sell his Model T motorcar to

47

a wealthy widow the next town over, for which Everett shed a tear while no one was looking, and there were many other things they'd grown quite used to which quickly became luxuries they could no longer afford.

By the time December arrived, Father and Watson still hadn't found any work. Sure, they'd found several odd little jobs here and there, but nothing that compared to having once owned a grocery store. On Tuesdays, Father drove the wealthy widow who'd bought his Model T to her bridge game, and she gave him a quarter for his trouble, and every so many weeks Old Mrs. Mulberry paid Watson to rake her leaves and chat with her over a cup of coffee. Though it's impolite to wish misfortune on others, Father and Watson made the most money when their neighbors — particularly the old ladies — had some sort of household difficulty. There were plumbing problems, clogged gutters, fallen trees, flooded basements, fireplaces in need of cleaning, and Father and Watson were there to offer aid the minute such things occurred. But being very neighborly to begin with, Father and Watson wished they could have lent their help for free, and could never bring themselves to charge much money for such services.

The December air was quite bitter that year, and the Swope house became a very chilly place to be. They could only afford a very little bit of coal, and so a fire became an after dinner treat for only the most wintery of evenings. To keep warm, Mother quilted several extra blankets for atop their beds, and the children played all day long so as not to let their blood grow cold. They also spent a lot more time cuddling with Poncho, which the dog didn't seem to mind in the least.

Charles and Everett had found they weren't very excited for Christmas that year with things being less spirited around the house. They'd helped Mother to decorate a Christmas tree with candles, bows, and little paper cutouts she'd helped them to make, but Charles especially thought that Mother seemed sad, which was not like her at all.

"Don't go asking her why she's sad now," Everett had told him. "It'll only make her sadder if she thinks you've noticed."

But Charles couldn't help himself, and when he'd asked Mother if she was sad, she'd sighed heavily and said, "No, my dears — not sad, but it does gladden a Mother's heart so to give her children a nice Christmas, and I expect we won't be able to afford much in the way of presents this year."

Everett, who was now quite angry with Charles, had replied, "But that's okay, Mother — we don't like presents all that much anyhow!" which was a lie, but the harmless sort of lie you tell mothers to keep them from crying.

"That's right," said Charles. "My watercolor set still has some paint left in it, and Everett's fire truck will be as good as new with some mending (for it had lost a wheel earlier that week). We don't need any presents, you see, so you needn't be unhappy!"

Mother had smiled at them and blinked back a few tears. "You two are the *dearest* children a mother could ask for," she said, and Charles and Everett felt quite pleased with themselves for having cheered her up.

Christmas day then arrived soon after to find them all in good spirits, and Charles and Everett went with Father to the butcher shop to help him pick out some chicken legs for Christmas supper. The butcher, however, had been so friendly and cheerful that he gave them a whole chicken instead, and they each wished him many happy Christmases before departing. Mother then fixed them a wonderful Christmas dinner with roasted chicken, cranberries, beans, and a spice cake for dessert, for which Watson had contributed the sugar with a portion of his leaf raking wages. After supper they all helped with the dishes, and then Mother played Christmas carols on the piano while they sang along. Watson in particular sang quite beautifully, and Charles and Everett begged him to sing "Good King Wenceslas", for it was their favorite.

Owing to the special occasion, a fire was lit, and they pulled the furniture close so they could warm themselves together and tell stories. Father told an especially good one about a man named Scrooge who called Christmas a "Humbug" and was then visited by three ghosts who made him realize how awfully jolly Christmas truly was — I hope you've been told this one before, for it's really one of the most wonderful stories you'll ever hear.

The children were having such a happy Christmas that they hadn't given even the slightest thought to presents, but after Father had finished the story, he pulled two big red stockings out from underneath the Christmas tree. There was one for Charles and another for Everett, and there was also a little bone tied up with ribbon for

Poncho. Baby Isabelle, who was not forgotten, was currently in Mother's arms gnawing on a new teething ring.

"But I thought we weren't to have any presents this year," said Everett, though he was looking quite anxious to dig through his stocking.

"Just a little something ..." said Mother, sweetly.

"That's right," said Father. "It's impolite to question a gift — now tuck in!"

And so the boys did as they were told, eagerly emptying the contents of their stockings onto the floor. Mother and Father had wrapped them each a gift in newspaper — for Charles, a book for his very own from Father's bookshelf about a shipwreck which Father had read himself as a boy, and for Everett, a model airplane just like one Father had taken them to see in which the Wright Brothers had taught army officers how to fly. There was also for each of them a pack of pencils, and in the foot of their stockings, an orange.

"Oh, thank you, thank you!" said the children collectively, admiring their gifts. Charles then exclaimed that this was the jolliest Christmas he could recall, and that he wished the Ku Klux people could see them having such a nice Christmas, because then they'd learn that it doesn't pay to be mean to people. This is quite true, and for those of you feeling very angry about the Swopes's burned down grocery store, you should know that they weren't about to let mean people make them unhappy for long, and you shouldn't either.

Snow fell outside their windows that evening as Christmas came to a close, and the next day Coopstown was a blanket of white, and the day after that, and many more days to follow. Charles and Everett exhausted themselves all winter making snowmen, building igloos, and having snowball fights with Bobby, Jimmy, Dotty, and the other neighborhood children until all the snow upon the ground had quite melted.

The warmth of spring then brought work upon Mr. Cooper's farm for Father and Watson. As it turned out, Mr. Cooper had no qualms delivering pumpkins to a black man, and when he'd found out what Mean Old Barney Lucas had done, he'd decided to find his delivery services elsewhere. But work on a farm involved long strenuous days for Father and Watson, and as kind as Mr. Cooper was, he could only afford to pay them a very little amount, but it was at least enough to buy coal for the chillier evenings and a pair of new leather shoes for Everett when he'd outgrown his old ones.

The months continued to fly by with very little excitement, that is until summer began and there arrived in the Swopes's mailbox a letter from Mother's sister, Elizabeth, in Massachusetts. Since it's no fun being told about letters, I'll let you read this one instead:

Dearest Mary, Edward, Everett, and Charles,

I do hope you are all coping in light of the unfortunate fate of Edward's grocery store. We think of you often, and wish we lived closer so as to lend a hand. I must now apologize for the irony of this letter, for instead of lending my own hand, I find myself in need of yours. You see, John and I have been called away on an archeological dig in Egypt — seems an ancient hidden city may have been discovered beneath the desert — and we'll be gone all summer. It's all been very short notice, and John and I are at a loss as to where to put Clara while we're gone. We were wondering if you might find it quite convenient to have her come stay with you? She'd be excellent company for Charles and Everett, and we'd pay you handsomely for the trouble (you mustn't argue on this matter!) I'm afraid we'd need you to meet her at the train station next Tuesday if you're willing. Do please reply with haste — we're quite in a bind.

Your ever loving sister,
Elizabeth (and John and Clara!)

P.S. Last week Clara broke Mother's porcelain figurine of the lady with a parasol. It was quite by accident of course, but I could have cried all evening! One can't blame children for these things though, I suppose.

Mother and Father read the letter several times over, but each time they finished they were no more keen on the idea of Clara coming to stay then they'd been to begin with. This was perhaps because they knew the girl to be at times overwhelming — not to mention she somehow managed to drag mud through the house every time she came for a visit. But how could they say "no" when Mother's sister was in such a dilemma? They knew they couldn't refuse, but this didn't keep the boys from trying to convince them otherwise when Father and Mother told them of the letter.

"But why can't Uncle John and Aunt Elizabeth take her with them?" asked Everett, trying his best not to whine. "I'm sure Clara would be much better suited to Africa."

"That's right," agreed Charles. "There'd be monkeys to play with and camels for her to ride and everything!"

Mother smiled. "Oh yes, for sure, but that's just it you see — little girls could find themselves in quite a lot of danger in Egypt if someone wasn't watching them all day, and I'm afraid your aunt and uncle will be much too hard at work to look after Clara."

"But surely they must have nannies in Egypt," suggested Everett, though Charles was less certain of this because he'd never read of any such things in books. Have you?

"Come now," said Father. "Let's not be disagreeable — the matter has already been decided. Families do things for one another from time to time, and this is just one of those things."

And so there was no more talk of whether or not Clara should come for a visit while her parents were in Egypt, though this did not stop Charles and Everett from griping about it whenever their parents were out of earshot.

"She hasn't got much for brains, that one," remarked Everett as politely as is possible to say someone hasn't got much for brains, and Charles agreed, remembering that the only books Clara had ever talked about were very light fluffy stories about princesses in towers.

"And she was very snively the last we saw her too," Everett added, which was quite true, seeing as her last visit Clara had been crying more often then not — and if there was one thing that Everett couldn't abide by, it was excessive crying.

The days preceding Clara's arrival seemed to pass quickly as Charles and Everett tried to make the most of what little Clara-free summer they had left. Charles's things were moved into Everett's room, which was perhaps the sorest subject of all for the boys, for they thought it was quite unfair that they should have to share a room all summer when Clara would have Charles's room all to herself.

"She'll be quite comfy, I expect," said Charles bitterly, shoving the last of his clothes into the wardrobe beside Everett's things.

"Well," said Mother, "we only have three bedrooms between us, and we can't very well chuck her in with Watson now, can we? So either you two share a room, or one of you will have to bunk with Clara."

This had put an end to Charles and Everett's grumbling, and then before they could hardly blink, Tuesday had arrived and Father had rented his old motorcar from the wealthy widow in order for them to fetch Clara from the train station. Mother had made the boys shine their boots and comb their hair, and they all stood upon the platform in their Sunday best awaiting the shrill peal of the train whistle as Clara came rolling into town.

Right on time, the train barreled into the station hissing and clanking and belching smoke. A few travelers carrying various accoutrements alighted from the passenger cars, and then there she was, clutching a crew member's hand and crying her little eyes out. It was just how Everett and Charles had expected to find her.

"My darling, whatever's the matter?" said Mother, rushing to embrace the girl. Meanwhile, Charles and Everett rolled their eyes.

The portly crew gentleman shoved the hanky with which he'd given Clara to wipe her tears back into his pocket. "She'll be right as rain in no time, Ma'am," he said, very gentlemanly-like.

"But what's upset her so?" asked Mother, wiping away a few stray tears from Clara's cheeks and kissing her upon the forehead.

"Thought she'd missed her stop, Ma'am, that's all," said the crew member, and then he handed over Clara's suitcase to Father and waved to them before hopping back onto the train.

Clara sniveled tragically. "It was a-awful, Auntie Mary — I walked all up and down the train car, but n-nobody c-c-could tell me where I was to get off," she cried, brushing her blonde curls out of her face, and straightening her pea coat. "I felt ever so alone ... you understand, don't you, Auntie dear?"

"Oh yes, of course," Mother commiserated, "but you're safe now, and we're delighted to see you — isn't that right?" Mother said to Charles and Everett.

Everett grumbled beneath his breath. "Yes ... very delighted," he said, and smiled as nicely as he could muster.

Charles then waved to his cousin, who was beginning to brighten. "Hello, Clara," he said.

Clara was apparently overcome with their enthusiasm, for she burst into fresh tears and threw herself at both Charles and Everett in a hug. "Oh! That's so kind of you!" she wailed. "It'll be wonderful having friends for the summer!"

Charles and Everett were still at the age when most boys feel the need to squirm away from girlish affection as though they may catch a virus, but Clara had a tight hold of them.

"Alright now," said Mother, noticing the boy's discomfort. "Let's head home for supper — you must be starving after your journey, Clara."

"Oh, yes," she said, releasing Charles and Everett. "They had the most awful food on the train!"

But Clara apparently didn't find Mother's cooking much better than the US Railway's, for that evening at supper she stirred her shepherd's pie around and around on her plate, only nibbling a bite full or two every now and then because she *was* terribly hungry.

"Why, Clara, you've hardly eaten," said Mother after everyone at the table had grown quite tired of hearing Clara's fork scrape across her plate. "Do you not like shepherd's pie?"

Clara blushed beneath her curls. "Usually, I do," she said, shyly. "Cook makes a delicious shepherd's pie!" She then stared ominously down into her plate and added, "I expect it's quite difficult to make."

Charles and Everett were outraged, and began shoveling forkful after forkful of the pie into their mouths to show how much they liked it, but Mother was unruffled by Clara's distaste for her cooking. "Well," she said, politely, "we usually eat what's on our plates, but I'm sure I can fix you up something else this once if you'd like. We want you to be comfortable."

Clara stopped stirring and put her fork down with a clatter. "Oh, thank you, Auntie dear! I'd like that very much."

Luckily, it turned out Mother could make a cold meat sandwich like Clara requested almost as well as "Cook", which was high praise from the girl indeed. Then after supper, Mother made them cups of hot cocoa (Clara's was "a bit warm" at first), and they played Parcheesi upon the kitchen table. Albeit mentioning several times that *her* family played the game slightly differently, Clara was almost cheerful and they quite enjoyed themselves — that is until it became clear that Charles would win, and Clara began to sigh heavily and look rather bored. It seemed as though she liked losing just as much as she had liked Mother's shepherd's pie.

With the arrival of bedtime, Charles and Everett were much less argumentative about going to sleep than usual, and they hurried up the stairs to their room without delay.

"Have you ever met a more snively, disagreeable child in all your life?" moaned Everett once they were behind the safety of his bedroom door.

"I dare say not," replied Charles, who was in the process of untying his boot strings.

Everett sighed and pulled on his pajamas before slipping under the covers. "I fear it's going to be an awfully long summer," he said.

"Oh, I don't know ... I expect it'll be nicer than having to go to school at least," said Charles, having inherited more of his Mother's optimism than had his brother.

"Just barely," croaked Everett.

Mother then entered the room to tuck them in and kiss them goodnight, and Charles and Everett told her how very much *they* liked her shepherd's pie no matter what Clara thought.

"I'm glad," she said, "but you two best be kind to Clara now ... I think she just needs a little time to adjust." And before they could crack any wise remarks, Mother switched off the light and left the room.

The boys began to nod off, and Everett had started to dream about a Parcheesi game in which Clara was wearing a turban and shouting "Hooray!" and Charles and Everett were sobbing into their handkerchiefs, when suddenly they awoke to the sound of voices coming from across the hall.

"It's okay, dear," Mother was saying gently. "You'll soon get used to things around here, and we'll all have a nice summer."

Then they heard Clara sniff, and sniff again. "I-I-I suppose I'm j-just missing my mummy and d-daddy, that's all," she said in between sobs.

Charles and Everett sat up in their beds and exchanged wide-eyed looks of disbelief.

"Get a load of that, will you," whispered Everett. "Good grief!"

And they both turned over and went back to bed.

In Which A Gypsy And A Dog Tell Fortunes At The Fair

In case you've placed my book down or had a good snooze since finishing the previous chapter, let me remind you that cousin Clara has come for a visit. Charles and Everett have certainly not forgotten. They have their oatmeal for breakfast, and she wants oatmeal too; they paint with Charles's watercolor set, and she wants to paint too; they say they're going to play in the old motorcar, and she says she'd like to come play too, and their mother is standing there all along making sure they don't do or say anything that might make their dear cousin feel unwanted.

"Fine," said Everett the morning after Clara's arrival in answer to her wanting to play in the motorcar, "but you'll have to ride in the rumble seat. Girls can't drive."

"*Everett*," said Mother sternly, narrowing her eyes at him as she pinned a diaper onto baby Isabelle.

Everett huffed, having momentarily forgotten his mother was still in the room. "Oh, alright — so girls *can* drive, after all," he conceded, "but they have to be properly licensed the same as the rest of us, and that took Charles several months, so there won't be any driving for you today."

Mother didn't quarrel with this, for she knew Everett would play fair eventually, and the children trotted out the back door heading for the motorcar with Poncho following close behind. They fledged through the tall grass of the field, feeling beads of perspiration form across their foreheads as they ascended the hill, swatting away the occasional encounter with a bug. Upon the crest sat the motorcar, gleaming handsomely beneath the warm summer sun.

"Oh, what a lovely car!" cried Clara, running up alongside it and skimming her hand across its shiny metal hood.

Before Everett could scold Clara for smudging the paint, Charles stopped in his tracks and said, "Clara — what did you just say?"

Clara pulled her hand away from the car and fiddled nervously with the pleat of her dress. "I said, 'Oh, what a lovely car'."

But Clara *hadn't* said "Oh, what a lovely car" — I just had to write it that way so you'd know what I meant. In truth, she'd said something more like "Oh, what a lovely *cah*."

Everett quickly knew what his brother was getting at. "Say, 'car' again," he ordered.

"Cah," repeated Clara. The word sounded quite like the sound you make when the doctor asks you to stick out your tongue, only with a "c" in front of it.

"Just as I thought," said Charles. "You're saying it wrong."

"I am not!" said Clara, looking quite harassed.

"I say — she certainly is," said Everett in agreement. "Say it again, only this time put the 'r' on the end of it. It's pronounced 'cahr'," he said in a perfect demonstration. (I do hope this is how you say it).

"*Cerr*," replied Clara, rounding her lips quite unnaturally.

Both Charles and Everett shook their heads. "No, that's not right at all," said Charles. "Try again."

"*Ch-or*," tried Clara most ardently after a moment's hesitation.

"No, no — definitely not," said Everett.

"*Cah-r*!" Clara nearly shouted at him in frustration, and sensing her near success, she then repeated herself much more plainly this time. "Car."

Charles nodded in approval, and Everett sighed, drawing the back of his hand across his forehead. "*Whew*! That's a relief," he said. "We thought there was something really wrong with you!"

Charles and Everett, however, weren't aware that people in Boston, Massachusetts often pronounce "car" this way, as with other words like "park" and "yard", in which they pronounce "paak" and "yaad". It's awfully tiresome to listen to if you don't live in Boston, but Clara did live there. She'd likely picked up the dreadful habit from other children in school, for by birth she was quite as British as Charles and Everett. Had I mentioned this? Well, if not, let me fill you in. Clara moved to America with her parents when she was about five or six years old. Her parents were both archeologists, you see, and they'd been offered teaching positions at a prestigious university in Boston. Coincidentally, the reason the Swopes later moved to America was largely because Mother couldn't bear being separated from her sister by an entire ocean. But I digress. I do apologize if I neglected to inform you of Clara's nationality. I hope you haven't been reading her lines with an American accent, because she'd hate that!

With Clara's linguistics sorted out, the children hopped into the car, Poncho in between Charles and Everett up front, and Clara obediently behind them in the rumble seat. If you don't know what a rumble seat is, it's quite like a back seat, only it sort of pops out of the trunk, and it's a lot more fun to ride in. You won't find them in cars nowadays though. Isn't that sad?

Everett hopped back out. "Forgot to start the engine," he said, slipping out of sight as he yanked on the hand crank at the front of the car. It made its usual ripping noise, but as for starting, the car required the children's imaginations as always.

"There she goes!" yelled Everett over the din of engine noises Charles was dutifully making at the back of his throat.

"Oh, how exciting!" cried Clara, her curls bouncing about her shoulders as their journey got off to a bumpy start.

As usual, Everett asked "Where to?", but while Charles and Clara were busy contemplating this question, he suddenly stopped making engine noises and took his hands off the wheel. "Oh, this won't do," he said.

Perhaps it was the heat of the day, or the presence of Clara, but for some reason or another, Everett wasn't in the mood for pretend driving. He was quite tired of the car never actually starting, and he thought it was high time they found something *real* to do.

"What's the matter with you?" said Charles in surprise.

"This is just silly, that's what," Everett replied. "Here we are with an entire summer ahead of us, and we're sitting in a broken down car making silly noises like simpletons."

"It's never bothered you before," Charles argued.

"Well it does now," said Everett. He slouched back in his seat looking ponderous, his eyes fixed upon the horizon. "What we need is an adventure!" he declared.

"What sort of adventure?" said Charles. "We haven't any money."

Everett gave this some thought. "I've got it!" he said finally. "If we haven't any money, why don't we do something to make some?"

Clara looked excited, but it took so little to excite her, and Charles was mulling this thought over in his head. "That's not half bad," he agreed. "We could make money to help Father! *Hmm*, but what could we do?"

"Let's give it a good think," said Everett, and so they each thought some more, though neither Charles nor Everett paid any attention to Clara's suggestion that they make their own jewelry. Even Poncho appeared to be thinking, that is until a fly decided to perch on the tip of his long white nose and distracted him.

They sat in quiet for a long time while a warm breeze wafted pleasantly in and out of the car. Then, breaking his train of thought, Everett thought he heard the faint hint of a melody floating through the air.

"Stop that humming!" he barked at Charles.

"It's not *me*," Charles shot back.

"Fine," said Everett, "then, Clara — stop that humming!"

"I wasn't humming ... honest," she said.

"Well it certainly wasn't me," said Everett indignantly.

"*Shh*," said Charles, and he stared out over the edge of the field while the other two reluctantly obeyed. "It wasn't any of us," he said. "*Look!*"

Everett and Clara followed the direction of Charles's finger until they spotted the top of a red cloth tent in the distance at the bottom of a hill.

"The music's coming from down there," said Charles, and sure enough, upon a closer listen, they heard what sounded like a fiddle and an accordion playing a sort of gig.

"It must be a fair!" said Clara, happily. "Oh, I love a good fair! Can we go? Please?"

Charles echoed Clara's enthusiasm. "We might be able to make some money there," he said. "Fairs are full of talented people trying to make money."

"Yeah, but which of us has any talent?" asked Everett.

Naturally, Clara eagerly volunteered. "I can do a cartwheel!" she said. "I did a really good one once — my feet went over my head and everything!"

"Isn't that the whole point of a cartwheel?" said Charles.

"Well, sure, but I'd just like to see you try one," she replied defensively.

"What does it matter?" said Everett. "Nobody's going to pay to see Clara do a cartwheel when there'll already be women walking tightropes and men breathing fire. We'll have to come up with something much cleverer than that."

And so they went back to thinking, all except for Poncho who yawned in boredom and flopped down upon the seat, his tongue dangling over the edge.

Everett grimaced at the string of drool that nearly landed on his shoe, but just then a light-bulb went off in his head, and his face broke into a smile. "I've just had an idea!" he shouted.

"*Oooh*, so have I," said Charles, impatiently. "Let me go first, please! Wait — oh no! I've forgotten it already."

"Never mind that," said Everett, and Charles frowned. "Since none of us have any talent, why don't we sell *pets*."

"*Pets*?" said Charles. "But the only pet we have is Poncho, and we couldn't possibly sell him," he said, grabbing the dog protectively.

"No! You didn't let me finish. Not *sell* him," said Everett, "we'll charge people to pet him! People are always saying how cute and friendly he is, and no one can see him without wanting to pet him ..."

"But we couldn't charge people for something like that," said Charles. "Could we?"

"Sure we can! People pay for pony rides all the time, and ponies aren't half as cute as Poncho."

"Well, *I* think it's a wonderful idea!" said Clara, though neither Charles nor Everett were at all surprised by this. "And we're such dear little children that people will be happy to give us their money."

"We'll see about that," said Everett, "but it's worth a try. Come on!" he said. He hopped out of the car and tore off in the direction of the fair, leaving Charles and Clara breathless to keep up with him with their shorter legs. Poncho was running ahead of Everett, barking as if to tell them all to hurry it along, and when Clara later tripped, he sprinted back and ran circles around her until she'd rejoined the herd.

The red tent grew larger and larger and the music louder and louder until it seemed as though the fiddle player was only a few feet away. The children skidded to a halt, hunched over and gasping for breath.

"Will you look at that!" said Everett as they peered down the final slope of grass at the colorful scene below. Scattered around the large red tent were swarms of noisy adults and children, shouting and screaming and roaring with laughter as they took in every inch of the fair.

"It's beautiful!" cried Clara, and it truly was a sight to see. There was a man juggling knives while riding a unicycle, a leopard in a cage, a fortune telling gypsy, a woman performing swinging acrobats upon a high metal bar, a puppet show, fire wielding dancers, and all the delicious candy and food you could imagine. Clara wanted a candy apple, and Charles some popcorn, but Everett quickly reminded them that they were there to make money, not to spend it.

They trotted down the hill and past a crowd of gentlemen playing marksmen games with air guns, coconuts, hoops, and horseshoes in attempts to win their lady friends the usual stuffed prizes.

"Where shall we set up?" said Charles.

"How about next to the gypsy?" suggested Everett. "Everyone will go and hear their horrific fortunes from her, and then they'll want to pet a nice big dog to cheer themselves back up."

"Good thinking," said Charles.

So they headed toward the gypsy's fortune telling booth, grabbing Clara when she got distracted by a hypnotist, and they parked Poncho in front of the red tent, which they discovered housed the grisly remains of some sort of ice man. Everett waved very business-like to the gypsy while she wasn't busy gazing into her crystal ball, and she glared at them suspiciously and returned the wave with a brief flash of her snaggletooth.

"Okay, so we'll need some sort of sign to advertise him," said Everett as Poncho panted happily beside him.

"But we haven't any paper or sheets of card," said Clara.

"We could write on my handkerchief," said Charles helpfully, whipping the shiny white linen from his pocket.

"Perfect," said Everett. "Now all we need is something to write with ... some ink or paint."

"There's a lady face painting over there," said Clara, pointing to a wiry-haired woman beside the candy apple stand. "I bet she'd let us borrow some paint!"

"Wonderful, Clara. Thank you!" beamed Everett. "You both wait here while I go and ask her," he said, grabbing for Charles's handkerchief and slipping out of sight.

Meanwhile, Clara smiled and felt all giddy inside, for she'd done something helpful and Everett had been kind to her.

Several minutes passed in which the gypsy continued to stare mistrustfully at Charles and Clara, and then Everett returned brandishing the handkerchief, now resplendent with large black writing. "She let me borrow her paint — though we have to let her pet Poncho for free when she goes on her break," he told them, holding out the handkerchief for them to read.

"*Poncho the Great Pyrenees — five cents a pet*," Charles read aloud, ignoring Everett's having misspelled pyrenees with a "z", which was quite wrong. Everybody knows that.

"Such nice writing," said Clara, repaying Everett's earlier kindness. The thing about Clara was that if you were nice to her for only a moment, she'd spend the rest of the day trying to be kind back, which was really a wonderful quality if only she didn't wreck it by crying so much.

This compliment earned Clara the duty of holding out the handkerchief for eager customers to see, and Charles was instructed to hold out his hat for collecting the money.

"Now all we have to do is wait for the money to start rolling in," said Everett, rubbing his hands together in anticipation. Poncho then barked as if to announce that he was open for business, and he sat wagging his tail back and forth looking quite ready for the petting to commence.

At first people seemed eager to pet Poncho — a man with twin daughters had gladly paid fifteen cents for them to play with the dog a few minutes, and Poncho had appreciatively showered the girls with kisses. Another family with three children then wanted to pet him because their own family dog had just died and they quite missed his company. However, upon hearing this story, Clara was reduced to tears, and she'd insisted the family not be charged because it was all so tragic. From then on, it seemed their luck was running out. People were much more inclined to simply smile at the children and *ooh* and *ahh* over Poncho from afar than to pay the five cents to pet him.

"Maybe we're not drawing enough attention," said Everett after while, and when they all agreed, he began to shout. "Get your pets! Come pet Poncho, the Great Pyrenees!" He said this as if it were a magician's name, like "Alonzo, the Magnificent" or "Catherine, the Great" — oh wait, that last one was a queen, not a magician. But you see what I mean, don't you? It was very clever advertising on Everett's part. "Only five cents a pet! Pet's for Poncho — get your pets!" he continued to shout.

This had helped a little, for two young children licking ice creams had heard Everett shouting, and when they'd spotted Poncho looking all adorable and cuddly, they'd yanked on their parents' shirt sleeves until they were handed the money to pet him. But Everett's shouting soon got on the gypsy's nerves, and she stormed over to them in a blaze of billowy fabric and jingling bracelets wearing a most disagreeable expression.

"Can't you children be quiet?!" she yelled, momentarily forgetting about her bogus Hungarian accent. "You're disrupting my aura!"

"Oh yeah?!" Everett yelled back. "Well—"

"We're sorry, ma'am," Charles interjected, stepping in front of Everett with a shove. "We won't shout any longer."

The gypsy glowered at them beneath her clumps of heavy black eyelashes. "Thank you," she said thickly, and stormed back to her fortune telling booth.

"What'dya do that for?" said Everett, rubbing the place where Charles had elbowed him. "I could have handled her."

"That's what I was afraid of," said Charles. "We don't want to get kicked out of the fair, do we? We've hardly made any money yet."

"Yeah, about that," said Everett, still scowling, "I think we need to go to plan B."

"But we haven't a plan B," said Clara.

"Exactly," said Everett, "but I have something up my sleeve."

They huddled close while he whispered his plan to them, and when he'd finished they ran off toward home, returning to their spot beside the gypsy an hour later with a completely different tactic.

This time when they parked Poncho in front of the red tent, he was wearing Father's uncle's turban, and the children were toting a piece of card displaying the words THE AMAZING DOGGY SWAMI TELLS YOUR FORTUNE! 10 ¢. Charles had been the one to come up with the name, having just read a buried treasure story set in India, and the others thought it sounded very exciting.

"He looks ever so smart in his turban," said Clara. "And it's such a lovely shade of lavender."

"It's not lavender — it's periwinkle," Charles corrected.

"I'm sure I saw a gum-ball that color once, and my father called it *lavender*," Clara insisted, stubbornly.

"Lavender's a flower, silly. It can't be a color," said Charles, feeling surer of this than he had anything else all day.

Clara's eyes brimmed with angry tears. "Just because it's one thing doesn't mean it can't be another," she argued. "A periwinkle isn't just a color either! Mother read me the strangest story about a periwinkle once."

"That wasn't a periwinkle — that was *Rip* Van Winkle!" Charles nearly shouted, for if there was one thing he couldn't tolerate, it was literary incorrectness.

Clara whimpered, her cheeks flushed, and she sobbed into Poncho's fur.

"Oh, don't start that again!' said Everett in disgust. "We haven't time for tears and arguments. Mop up then, and we'll get started," he added, throwing his handkerchief at her.

For the first time in all her life, Clara felt a twinge of embarrassment at her tears, and was compelled to dry them quickly and call a truce with Charles, which Charles accepted immediately if only to keep her from crying again.

Ignoring their reconciliation, Everett began to write on another piece of card with a brush and paint they'd brought from home. "Now," he said, "we need to come up with some fortunes for Poncho to point to with his paw ... you know, like 'Mortal Danger' and 'Financial Fortune'."

"Those are good ones, write those down," said Charles, and Everett began to paint.

"How about 'True Love'?" Clara suggested.

"Good, good — any more?" said Everett.

"Maybe 'New Job'," said Charles. "Father could use one of those."

Everett added that one too and then dropped the paint brush into the can. "Alright then, we're ready to go!" He straightened the turban atop Poncho's head and began to shout once more. "Come see the Amazing Fortune Telling Doggy Swami! Ten cents a fortune! Come and get 'em!"

The gypsy instantly looked up from her crystal gazing and wrung her hands in fury. But before she could stomp over to the children's booth, a crowd of eager fair-goers had swarmed around Poncho, pointing and standing on tippy-toe to get a good look. Even the gypsy's customer leapt up in the middle of her reading to run and join the quickly growing line.

"Charles, get your hat ready," said Everett in excitement. "First customer, please!" he called to the crowd.

A man toward the front raised his hand and stepped forward, placing a dime in Charles's hat.

"The Amazing Doggy Swami will now read your fortune," said Everett majestically, and all eyes turned to Poncho. "Please place out your hand," Everett instructed, and the man did as he was told. Poncho yawned and blinked a few times, and then leaned his nose in to sniff the man's fingers, finally giving them a lick.

"Clara — the Board of Fortunes, if you please," said Everett, and Clara placed the piece of card in front of the dog.

For a moment, the children held their breath, hoping the dog wouldn't wreck their plan by lying down or eating the paper, and the crowd grew increasingly rowdy as nothing in particular continued to happen.

But then, as if he'd been waiting for a mystical sign, Poncho plopped his paw firmly down upon "Financial Fortune".

"And there you have it, folks — the Amazing Doggy Swami has spoken! This gentlemen will have financial fortune in his future."

The man bowed to Poncho and thanked him over and over again until he was pushed out of the way by a portly, handsome woman with an alligator handbag, anxious for her own fortune.

"Well, what'll it be?" she bellowed at the dog. "True love, I hope," she cooed.

"Not likely," said Everett under his breath.

"What was that boy?" she said, whipping her head around to squint at him.

"Eh-hem, yes, well — let's just ask the Amazing Doggy Swami!" choked Everett. "Your hand, please, madame."

The woman held out her plump jeweled fingers, and Poncho instantly gave them a lick. The crowd grew quiet as they awaited the dog's prediction.

Poncho's head bobbed up and down at the sight of a butterfly, and then, as if out of boredom, he plopped his paw down upon "Mortal Danger".

The woman gasped and clutched her handbag to her chest. "Oh — well, I'm sure this is all in good fun ... a dog can't predict the future ... right?" she said, eyeing the children desperately. But the crowd backed away from her like she was the plague, and she hiccuped and scurried out of sight in a panic.

"Do be careful!" called Everett gleefully, and Charles and Clara smiled at each other as another dime was dropped into the hat.

This time a young man stepped forward, nervously wringing a folded newspaper in his hands.

"C-could the dog tell me what's in m-my future, please?" he said, sticking out a shaking hand for Poncho to lick.

"Of course," Everett assured him, "he's the Amazing Doggy Swami!"

Poncho barked importantly, and the man leapt back in surprise, wiping sweat from his brow. The dog blinked several times at him, and then without delay placed his paw squarely upon "True Love".

The crowd cheered wildly, and the man broke into a grateful smile, reaching out to pet the dog.

"*Ah-ah*!" chirped Everett with an outstretched hand. "Not while he's working."

"Oh, yes, of course. Thank you — thank you!" said the man, bowing happily as he slipped back into the crowd.

"Next!" cried Everett, and Charles held out his hat as at least a dozen more customers took their turns having Doggy Swami predict their futures, the only disruption being the occasional need for Clara to straighten his turban.

Though the children had never really thought Poncho could predict the future, they began to wonder when several customers came rushing back throughout the day with wild stories of success. These stories did nothing for the gypsy's business, and she appeared to be playing solitaire with her tarot cards, occasionally turning up her lip in Doggy Swami's direction and muttering under her breath.

Their very first customer, whose fortune had entailed financial success, came bustling back through the crowd waving a wad of green bills in the air.

"That dog's the real thing! He really is!" the man cried. "I guessed the right number of jelly beans and won twenty dollars! And then, not two minutes later, I put my coin down on the number twenty-four, and blast if the darned wheel didn't land right on it! Won me'self another twenty dollars!"

The children eyed Poncho curiously, but the crowd roared in excitement, and more and more customers pushed their way into the line. Soon after, the nervous fellow who'd received the prediction of "True Love" galloped to the front of the crowd looking as giddy as a racehorse, his arm slung around the shoulders of a very lovely girl with a pretty pink hat and rosy red cheeks.

"Someone give that dog a biscuit!" he hooted. "I've met her — my one true love!"

The girl he was wrapped around broke into a fit of giggles. "We're getting *married*," she gushed.

If possible, the crowd's excitement grew even more feverish, and Charles's hat became so filled with coins that he was finding it dreadfully heavy to hold. There were then many more testimonials of Doggy Swami's ability as the day wore on, including one by the handsome lady with the alligator purse who'd pummeled her large frame back through the hoards of people, dabbing at her shiny round face with a lace handkerchief.

"I tell you — I've just seen my life flash before my eyes!" she wailed. "I was enjoying the juggling act over there (she pointed) when suddenly the juggler lost control and a bowling pin came hurdling through the air straight for my head! If the gentleman sitting beside me hadn't leapt up and caught it just in time, I'd surely be dead!" she said, which was probably an exaggeration, but a happy customer was a happy customer, as the saying goes.

Soon the children were just as convinced of Poncho's powers as the crowd was, though they had no idea how he'd gotten them. The hat and their pockets were bursting with coins, and Clara had even begun to collect them in the fold of her skirt, but the dog showed no signs of growing weary from all his predictions. He continued to dish out fortunes until the gradually thinning crowd became distracted by some loud noises and shouting.

The children turned to see the gypsy violently beating a tambourine and chanting something in another language. She scurried up to them, still wildly beating and chanting, and looking awfully sinister with her bulgy eyes and hairy mole.

Giving the tambourine a final shake, she leaned forward, leering at them. "I just put a curse on you, and all your children!" she hissed.

Poncho growled, ready to attack should she come any closer.

"But we haven't any children," said Everett firmly, though his insides felt like jelly.

The gypsy stamped her foot, and she jingled from head to toe. "That's beside the point, boy! I curse your future children then. Now get lost — and take that confounded mutt with you! If I ever set eyes upon you round these parts again, I'll turn every last one of yeh's into toads!"

The children cowered for a moment, not sure what to do, but when the gypsy erupted a moment later, screaming and banging upon her tambourine, they had no choice but to grab Poncho and run with all their might, coins flinging in every direction as they were chased from the fair.

In Which Doggy Swami Goes To The Races

"Now what do we do?" said Charles once they'd made it back to the motorcar and caught their breath.

"Well we can't go back there," said Everett, staring bitterly back in the direction of the fair. "How much money have we got left?" he asked, fearing that the majority of it had been lost in their escape.

Charles shook his hat and it jingled half-heartily, and Clara gazed down into the folds of her dress, which she'd been holding out in front of her, to find three lonely dimes amidst the fabric.

"Oh, this is awful," she said. "There had to have been dozens of dimes in here before that terrible gypsy chased us away."

"And my hat was so heavy I could barely hold it," said Charles.

"That wretched thing," muttered Everett, speaking of the gypsy. "We'd been doing quite well for ourselves till she stuck her ugly nose in ... could have had a good haul."

"I suppose we did sort of take away her customers," Clara admitted.

"Nonsense," said Everett. "It was just good business, that's all."

Poncho sighed miserably from the passenger seat of the motorcar where he'd curled up to rest. The turban had fallen off his head and was now laying on the floor of the car.

"You don't think she's *really* put a curse on us, do you?" said Clara.

"Course not silly — there's no such thing as curses," said Everett.

But Clara wasn't convinced, and by the looks of things, neither was Charles. He'd gulped and tried to loosen the collar round his neck.

"Well there's no sense in being miserable," Everett began. "I don't know about you, but I'm starting to think Poncho can really predict the future! Though I have no bloody idea how."

All three children turned to contemplate the dog, but he merely blinked at them and turned away.

"Maybe he ate some magic kibble," Clara suggested.

"Not likely," said Charles. "He always eats the same thing."

"I don't much care *how* he can predict the future," said Everett, "but it's lucky for us that he can. There must be loads of other places we could make money with a fortune telling dog."

"Like where?" said Clara.

"Well ..." said Everett, considering the matter. "I'm sure we can think of something."

And so, for the third time that day, they were all thinking again, which was quite a lot of thinking considering they weren't even in school.

"*I* know!" said Charles, excited to have beaten Everett this time. "We'll take him to the racetrack! Father says people are always betting too much money on horse racing, and then getting very upset when their horses don't win. I suspect they'd like to know who was going to win ahead of time."

This was such a brilliant idea that Everett couldn't argue, even though he liked it much better when he was the one coming up with ideas. "That'll do just fine," he said. "Really good thinking, mate!"

"But how will we get to the racetrack from here?" said Clara, which was a reasonable question.

Charles and Everett were silent a moment.

"We'll take the streetcar," said Everett. "We've plenty of money left to get downtown, and we're sure to make plenty more while we're there."

"Are we going to go now? It might be dark soon," said Clara.

"No, it's much too late. We'll have to wait till tomorrow," Everett replied. "Probably best, anyhow — I'm getting awfully hungry."

Both Charles and Clara agreed, as did Poncho, who hurried home quickest of all in hopes that his food bowl might be full when he arrived.

They ate their dinner quietly that evening while Mother and Father talked about their day, and when the children were asked what they had done, they didn't mention the fair or the gypsy or trying to make money, because they knew their parents would try to dissuade them, and they did so want to help.

Clara was much less snively when Mother put her to bed that night, and she found she was hardly homesick at all with a streetcar ride and the racetrack to look forward to with Charles and Everett.

The next morning, they quickly ate the waffles Mother had made them, and then pulled on their boots and headed for the door.

"Where are you three off to so early?" asked Mother, feeding baby Isabelle her bottle.

"Uh ... just going out to play!" said Everett.

"It's much nicer playing in the morning when it's not so hot," Charles cleverly added.

Mother looked at them suspiciously, but in the end she simply said, "Just don't go too far."

"We won't," they lied, though all three of them later felt pangs of guilt in the pit of their stomachs for this.

"*Tally ho* then, Mother," said Everett.

"What was that?" Mother called after them.

"Um — never mind. See you!" Everett called back, and they slipped out the door before she could say anything more.

"*Oh*, I hate lying!" Clara whined as they trotted around the side of the house and toward the road.

"I don't like it any better than you," said Everett, "but it was the only way we'd be able make some money for Father." He was holding the turban under his arm, and Poncho was keeping pace beside him.

They walked a quarter of a mile to the streetcar stop and waited until it came clanging and dinging down the middle of the road. You're probably not quite familiar with streetcars, and that's because not too many places have them any more, but they were a lot like trains, only much less big and not nearly so noisy. This one was swampy-green, and had a conductor named Frank who took a nickel fare each from the children as they boarded.

"Excuse me, sir — could you tell us how many stops till the racetrack?" said Everett.

"Three," replied the conductor, routinely. "Go on — take your seats. I'll let you know when to get off. And keep ahold of that dog." He scratched his whiskered chin and pressed something on the controls.

The children thanked him and found three seats together next to a woman wearing a rain bonnet. As the car began to carry on down the road, Poncho stuck his head out the window to sun himself and air out his tongue, and the children contemplated their mixed amount of excitement and fear at riding the streetcar without their parents' knowledge. Stops were made at the bank and pharmacy, and then the conductor shouted "Bel Air Racetrack!" and they alighted, waving to the gentlemen as the car pulled away.

They could already hear the roaring of a crowd and the bang of starting pistols as they traveled up the dirt path leading to the stadium. Parked motorcars lined the entrance, and many hotdog and sandwich vendors awaited the visit of hungry patrons between races. If they stood on their toes, the children could see over the white picket fence just well enough to spot the flash of horses as they rounded the bend.

"I'd love to ride a horse," said Clara, longingly.

"Not one of those, you wouldn't," said Everett. "You'd get thrown right off!"

Clara shrugged, and they made their way up a flight of stone steps till they found themselves looking down upon the grandstand at the mass of people spotted about the seats. Nobody was sitting, they were all on their feet cheering or jeering and waving hats and newspapers as the horses' hooves pounded in rhythm around the track.

The children made their way through the swarms of men in hats and business suits, all of whom were scouring the papers or swapping betting strategies and voicing superstitions. A collective cry of defeat was heard as the race came to an end and many cursed the loss of their week's wages upon a losing horse, but then with quickly rehabilitated confidence, they returned to the ticket counters in droves.

The children found a break in the crowd and stood on the back of some empty seats to get a look at the track. Seven perfectly groomed chestnut-colored horses with shiny black tails were led out of the paddock at the sound of the trumpeter's "call to post", and they paraded past the stands onto the track where they waited at the starting gate for the crack of the pistol to signify the beginning of the race. The jockeys in their different colored silks avoided talking to one another as they sat atop their respective horses, crouched in the starting position.

At the bang, a puff of smoke shot from the gun that'd been fired by a tiny fellow in stripes, and the horses thundered out of their gates, stirring a cloud of dust in their wake as they spread out around the track. Scores of noisy spectators screamed and hollered at their favorites to win, waving their hats and newspapers in excitement or frustration. Then in an instant, it was all over, and some of those men were now cheering wildly, while others were shaking their heads and entering heated conversations with those around them as they made another dash to the ticket counters.

"What fun!" cried Charles. "I can't wait for the next one to start!"

"Don't forget — we're here on business, not to watch the race," said Everett, and he gazed about their surroundings looking for a place to set Poncho down.

"Alright, let's set up over there," said Everett, pointing to a bare spot of wall beside the ticket line. "People can consult Poncho, and then buy their tickets." He whipped out his own handkerchief this time, which he'd painted on at home. It read, THE AMAZING DOGGY SWAMI PREDICTS THE WINNER! 10 ¢.

When they'd gotten into position and sat the turban snugly down atop Poncho's ears, Everett began to shout. His throat soon hurt however, because racetracks are noisy places, and a young boy can only yell so loudly. The children waited anxiously for customers to materialize, the smell of fried chicken and beer wafting around them as they stood as imposingly as possible by the line of gamblers in hopes of being noticed. Then, a jolly man with a round stomach saw Everett's handkerchief and said, "Ha! Aw, why not? He sure is cute." And so he handed them a dime, and Everett said, "Doggy Swami will now tell you the winner!"

But Clara nudged Everett in the side, and pulled him closer. "How's Poncho supposed to pick the winner?" she whispered. "His paw is much too big to point one out on the newspaper."

"Jeepers!" Everett hissed, and ran his fingers through his hair. "Why didn't you say something before?"

"Because I only just thought of it," she said.

"Em," Everett said to the gentleman, stalling till he could come up with something. "I will read the names of the horses and Doggy Swami will signal when I've read the winner's name," said Everett. "*I hope*," he added under his breath.

The man chortled, and took a drag from his cigar, and Everett asked to borrow his newspaper and began to read from the list of competing horses. "King Caramel!" he shouted, but hearing the first horse's name had no impact upon the dog. "Fire Monkey!" he continued, desperately. "Silver Thunder! Pickle Rocket! Dirty Laundry! Poppycock!" And still when there was nothing, Everett shouted the last name, "Uncle Pat's Revenge!" (Very silly names indeed, I admit, but people *will* name horses the strangest things!)

The children prayed that Poncho would not simply sit dormant beside them, but as of yet, he'd shown no indication that any psychic thought had passed through his tiny brain.

The gentleman began to laugh, his belly shaking up and down. "You kids need to work on your tricks," he said, slapping Everett on the back, but just then Poncho snapped his jaws as if trying to catch a fly and barked three times consecutively.

"He's made a prediction!" cried Charles, sounding much more surprised by this than he should have seeing as this was exactly what they'd said the dog could do.

Everett read down the newspaper to find the third name on the list. "It's no trick, kind sir! Doggy Swami has made his prediction. Silver Thunder will win!"

The man laughed again, and with a tip of his hat walked toward the ticket counter shaking his head in amusement. The children had no idea which horse he ended up betting on, but five minutes later when the race had finished, he came back to them looking wide eyed and scratching his head. "You know, that darn dog was right. What's he say about the next one?"

And so Everett read the list of horses in the next race to Doggy Swami, and in doing so caught the attention of several other betters. Two new gentlemen thought they'd give it a try, and Everett then heard a lady in an orange dress and very smart hat say, "How darling! Honey, give them a dime — they *are* cute children," which Everett winced at, but the couple quickly paid and Doggy Swami then predicted the winner by barking five times in succession. Delighted, the customers moseyed over to the ticket counter to place their bets, still smiling as though it was all just the most adorable little magic trick.

The horse race commenced and the crowds erupted in wild cheers as usual, though the children could not see the horses from where they were standing. But when it had ended, there was suddenly a swarm of people rushing toward them and screaming "We won! We won!", and they must have told everyone around them about Doggy Swami because there were now many more customers than before. Dozens of people were shoving their fists through the crowd to place dimes in Charles's hat so that they might be privy to Poncho's next prediction, which Clara later remarked was very fair of them because they could have just listened and not paid anything at all.

Another winner was announced, and this time the crowd stormed up to the ticket counters to collect their winnings and place wagers on the next race. Upon the starting pistol, the children waited while the crowd watched in anticipation. Meanwhile, two racetrack employees wearing green visors rounded the corner chatting to one another.

Everett put away his handkerchief.

"—The folks keep a'comin' up, and they're each of them bettin' for the same horse!" said the one employee. "No one's even placed a trifecta or a parlay in the whole last hour." These were words none of the children had ever heard before, but they hadn't time to ponder their meaning before the man continued, "Somethin's fishy, Mitch, I'm a'tellin' ya!" And then the two men walked through a door and out of sight.

The children smiled at one another, knowing that the "something fishy" was Poncho, but before they could speak, the crowd returned, bigger in number than ever before. Clara was once again forced to use the fold of her dress to hold all the excess dimes, and this time she vowed not to let any of them fall out. People packed in as close as they possibly could to the dog, who was completely unalarmed by the massive amounts of attention, and they peered over one another's shoulders and poked their faces through holes to listen for Doggy Swami's prediction.

Everett began calling out the names of the next set of competing horses. "Dixie Damsel! Cookie Cutter! Copper Penny! Sugar Princess! Flying Tomahawk! Salty Banana! and Ahoy Matey!" he shouted. There wasn't so much as a peep as the people awaited Doggy Swami's numeric barking system. But this time, when the dog opened his mouth, it was to sneeze, and the turban flew right off his head as he sneezed and sneezed again.

Many people laughed or made coddling noises. Everett quickly sat the turban back atop Poncho's head, but to the children's surprise, the dog wouldn't have any more of it, and he tipped the turban back off with his paw at once.

Nervously, Everett chose to leave the turban where it was and instead decided to read the names of the horses again. When he had finished, Poncho barked only once to announce that Dixie Damsel would win. The crowd again spirited themselves to the counters with money at the ready to place their bets, and then returned to the grandstand to await the next race.

While they had a minute free, Everett tried once again to sit the turban atop Poncho's head, but he repeatedly shook it off.

"I suspect he's grown tired of it," said Charles.

"It's probably heavy for him," agreed Clara.

"Oh well," said Everett.

A moment later the crowd again erupted with the end of the race, only this time there seemed to be quite an awful lot of booing. Before the children could ponder this, they were engulfed by crazed men and women shaking their fists at Poncho and claiming he'd been wrong. One woman even cried that she'd bet all her rent money on his last prediction.

Poncho looked as though he couldn't have cared less.

The children were alarmed — what did this mean? Everett tried to reason with the crowd. "Well, faulty predictions do happen now and again ... it was probably just the sneeze that threw him off. Give him another chance, do!"

The crowd quieted down quickly, and a handful of people reluctantly placed more dimes in the hat and waited to hear what Doggy Swami would predict next.

Everett read the next set of names from the newspaper, and without fail, Poncho barked four times, one right after the other.

"There you have it folks! A sneeze-free prediction! Leaping Buttercup will win the race!"

But Leaping Buttercup didn't win the race either. In fact, she came in last, and when the crowd returned in a symphony of thundering feet, they were looking more menacing and angry than ever, and were each demanding their money back.

Seeing as this was only the children's second day of running a business however, and they had no return policy, their only instinct was to run. Grabbing Poncho round the collar, they just barely managed to escape the cluster of outstretched hands and the hail of newspapers and pencils flying through the air. One foul looking woman even threw a half-eaten chicken leg, which managed to strike Clara in the back.

They were chased by several large-sized gentlemen, but being so much smaller, the children were able to slip in and out of the flocks of people much more swiftly, and after running for what felt like minutes, Charles, Everett and Poncho, stopped to catch their breath and get their bearings. In doing so however, they suddenly noticed that in addition to losing the angry mob, they'd also lost Clara somewhere along the way.

"Clara! CLARA!" they called, searching high and low for her.

"*You're* going to have to tell Mum and Dad we lost our cousin," said Charles.

Everett sighed. "She *would* lose herself, that one."

"You don't suppose one of those men caught her, do you?" asked Charles.

But there was no need to answer this question, for just then Everett spotted the tiny girl perched in front of a desk where a man sat holding a microphone and a pair of binoculars. She was crying and rubbing her eyes with her free hand (for she was still holding onto the fold of her dress, dear thing) and telling the man that she was lost. As Charles and Everett approached, she was in the middle of giving him their names, which he was scribbling down on a piece of notepaper, likely so he could make an announcement about a missing cousin over the speakers.

Before the damage could be done, they ran up to Clara, and she burst into fresh tears of relief and squeezed them both tightly.

"Oh, I'm such a silly fool!" she cried, hugging Poncho round the neck. Neither Charles nor Everett argued. "I'm sorry I got lost!"

"These the folks you were looking for, little missy?" asked the man behind the desk.

But Clara didn't have a chance to reply, for someone yelled "There they are! Over there!", and a man in the distance was pointing to the dog and three children, and motioning to the man with binoculars. "*Stop them!*"

There were now two ticket counter salesmen among the throng of angry gamblers chasing after the children, and with no time left to lose, Everett yanked Clara away by the wrist just as the man leapt at her over the desk, and they fled the stadium, ignoring the shouts of "Impudent Children!" and "Did you see that?!" as they shoved past the mass of patrons on their way out.

They ran so hard it felt like their hearts would implode within their chests, but miraculously the streetcar was just coming to a stop as they made it to the end of the dirt path, and they hopped aboard without a single glance over their shoulders.

"Oh, bless you! You're just in time," cried Clara, and without thinking she leaned in to give Frank the conductor a kiss on the cheek. They each then paid their fare with one of the many shiny coins they now possessed, and fell breathlessly into three empty seats with Poncho at their feet.

Looking rather pleased, Frank hit a button, and the streetcar pulled away.

In Which Baby Isabelle Says
A Whole Lot

When the children arrived back home around mid-afternoon, they paused outside the back door before entering the house.

"What are we going to do with all this money?" asked Charles, with the hat full of coins held out in front of him. "We can't go in with it like this."

"Hmm," said Everett. "Let's pour all the money into our shoes. Mother doesn't like us wearing them into the house anyway."

And so Charles emptied the contents of his hat into his boots, and Clara made a sort of funnel with her dress for the coins to slip through the fabric and into her own pair of shoes, clinking one after the other. Then, each holding a set of laces, the children walked into the house and set their shoes beside the doorway, casually greeting Mother who was in her rocking chair fiddling with a needle and thread.

"Oh, thank goodness you children are home. Sit with your baby sister for a bit, would you? I can't leave her unattended, and I must use my sewing machine," she said, holding out the lace veil she'd been embroidering for a young girl down the street whose wedding was in a few weeks. "I'll start supper in about an hour, so stay out of the cupboards!"

Mother then disappeared up to her sewing room, and the children were alone except for baby Isabelle.

"Let's count our money," said Everett, grabbing the three pairs of shoes and dumping their contents upon the floor. "Lucky we were able to hold on to most of it this time."

"Oh, Auntie Mary and Uncle Edward will be so pleased when we give it to them!" said Clara gleefully.

"We haven't near enough yet," said Everett, "but it's a good start. Plus, we can't go giving Mother and Father the money ourselves or they'll never take it, and they'd probably want us to return it too. We'll have to come up with some other way, but we can worry about that later."

Poncho laid down on the floor beside them while they began to count.

"Stop saying your numbers aloud, Clara!" said Charles shortly after. "I'm getting all mine mixed up."

"*Sorry*," she said, now mouthing the numbers instead. "Oh, look what you've done. Now I've lost track."

"Crikey," moaned Everett. "So have I."

They each tossed the coins they'd been counting back onto the pile. "This is going to take forever — there are so many!" said Charles.

"Just think how much *more* money we'd have earned if Poncho hadn't lost his powers," said Clara.

"Yeah, about that," began Everett. "I wonder why he stopped being able to make predictions. He had such a good run, and then all the sudden ... *poof*! Doesn't make a lick of sense, really." He stared pensively at the napping dog for a moment. "You don't think ... no, it couldn't be," he muttered.

"What?" said both Charles and Clara.

"Well, he only stopped predicting the future when the ... oh, but that's crazy," he said.

"What's crazy?" said Charles and Clara more impatiently this time.

"The idea of the *turban* granting special powers."

Charles and Clara's eyes grew to the size of saucers. "But that must be it!" cried Charles. "Father said his uncle could do all sorts of things when he was wearing the turban! That's got to be it!"

"Oh, come on," said Everett, shaking his head. "There's no such thing as a magic turban."

"Well it's not much crazier than a dog being able to predict the future in the first place!" Charles argued.

Everett considered this. "You know, you have a point there."

"I wonder what would happen if one of us put the turban on!" said Clara excitedly. "Maybe we'd have some sort of magical ability too."

But before they had time to ponder this, they heard footsteps coming down the stairs, and then Watson materialized in the kitchen wearing a pair of grass stained overalls.

The children tried to hide the coins, but there was no time.

"My! Where did you kids get all that money?" he said when he spotted the mound of dimes upon the floor.

"Um ... allowance!" said Everett, quickly.

"We've been saving it for years!" added Charles.

Watson eyed them skeptically, but to their great fortune, he wasn't inquisitive by nature, and asked no further questions.

"Well, I'm off to mow Mrs. Mulberry's lawn," he told them. "I'll see you all for dinner ... your mama's invited me down for pot roast. Right kind of her."

"That'll be nice," said Clara, who'd grown quickly fond of Watson.

"See you!" added Charles and Everett.

Watson then trudged out the back door swigging a bottle of ginger beer and humming tunelessly to himself, leaving the children alone once again.

"Let's count the money later," said Clara. "I want to see what else the turban can do!"

Of this they were equally curious, and so Everett gathered up the coins and dumped them back into their shoes, and Charles fetched the turban.

"I think we should test it out on baby Isabelle first, don't you?" said Everett.

All in agreement, they huddled around the bassinet while Charles attempted to sit the turban atop Isabelle's head. But the baby appeared dubious throughout the whole ordeal, and with good reason, for once Charles lowered the turban, it cast a shadow upon her pale crown, and then fell past her ears, covering her head completely and coming to rest upon her shoulders.

"She looks just like a martian!" cried Charles in delight. Undoubtedly, he'd just read a book about a martian. He was always relating things to books he'd read.

Clara very much agreed, but quickly said, "Oh, do take it off — she mightn't be able to breathe!"

Charles did so, and when baby Isabelle's head reappeared, she was looking rather surly.

"Well that won't do," said Everett.

"Maybe if we unraveled it and wrapped it round her like a diaper," suggested Clara.

The children had a go of this, and it worked quite nicely, but after several moments observation, nothing particularly magical had happened.

"Hmm," said Everett. "I suspect it's cause she's a baby. Babies can't have talent."

"But there must be things they wish they could do, even if they can't say so," said Clara.

The boys agreed, and Charles later confided to Everett that this was the wisest thing their cousin had said since her arrival, but still baby Isabelle neglected to display any significant talent.

They were just about to remove the turban-diaper when Isabelle began to cough as though she were choking, and then all of a sudden she babbled, "Blubba-de-blooper-do," or something quite like it.

The children exchanged curious glances. "I think that's the first time she's spoken, except to cry!" said Charles.

"Yes, but it wasn't actual words," said Everett.

"Maybe she's just learning to speak," said Clara. "Let's see if we can get her to say 'da da'. My mother says babies always say 'da da' first." So Clara lowered her face level with the baby's and made a silly expression. "Can you say 'da da'?" she cooed, overexerting her lips. "Come on cutie pie, say 'da da' for cousin Clara."

If Charles and Everett weren't quite mistaken, they'd swear baby Isabelle rolled her eyes. And then, as if this wasn't strange enough, she did the unthinkable. She *spoke* ... in sentences!

Specifically, she said, "Don't be ridiculous, child! Of course I can say 'da da'. Do I look like I was just born yesterday?"

Each of the children leapt back in surprise, looking as if some sort of alien had just invaded their dear baby sister. Her voice was not like a baby's at all — it was rather reminiscent of lady announcers on the radio or Mother when she was reading poetry, only Isabelle had a slight lisp seeing as her mouth was all gums.

"Well, *yes*, very nearly anyways," said Clara, who was perhaps feeling the bravest of all at the moment since it wasn't her own baby sister sassing her.

"Well, I wasn't!" snapped Isabelle, coldly. "And I don't appreciate your tone."

Clara hadn't known she'd used a tone, but there was clearly no room for discussion on the matter.

"Now listen you three, I have some demands. I'd like steak for dinner, and from now on I want fresh carrots! None of that mashed stuff."

"But you haven't any teeth!" said Clara in horror.

"That's not very nice," the baby retorted. "I'd rather not have any teeth at all than have awful crooked ones like yours."

Charles and Everett stifled a laugh, but Clara scowled and covered her lips with her hand, suddenly feeling embarrassed.

"What's so funny you two?" asked Isabelle, turning to her brothers. "I have a bone to pick with you, you know. How come you never ask me to go play in that old motorcar?"

Charles and Everett blinked in confusion. "But you're much too small!" they said. "You could get hurt."

"That's beside the point. It's just nice to be asked these things from time to time, you know?"

The boys gulped and nodded, for they could think of nothing else to say or do.

"Now help me out of this contraption here," she said, speaking of her bassinet, "I'd like to face the window a bit. Haven't seen the sun in days — it won't be long and I'll have prison pallor."

"How do you even know what that means?" said Charles, feeling quite affronted, for he'd only just learned that term a few months back when Bobby Smalls had pneumonia and started to look awfully pale from staying indoors all the time.

"Why shouldn't I know what it means? Do I look like I just fell off the turnip truck?" Isabelle scoffed.

All three children quickly shook their heads. "No, of course not! You look very, uh ... sophisticated," added Charles.

"Humph," said Isabelle, and the two boys then helped transport her over to the window in order to get some sun.

By this point, Poncho had awakened from his nap and become very interested in the overly talkative baby, and he leapt onto his hind legs to utilize his sensory skills of sniffing and licking.

"I wish you'd tell that beast to keep his tongue to himself. It's a hazard to my complexion," the baby spat.

Again, Charles marveled at her vocabulary, but he did not argue. "Down Poncho, down boy!" he said, and the dog fell back on all fours and wandered off looking as though his feelings had been hurt.

They held baby Isabelle in front of the window for quite some time while she took in the view and complained about the state of the garden, and then finally she told them she'd had enough.

"That'll do for now. Put me back. It must be getting time for tea — I'll have mine with a lump of sugar, if you please," she said, and when they hesitated, she added, "Get on with it then!"

Having learned not to question things, Charles put the kettle on, and Clara helped to prepare the tea service for four.

The children felt rather silly sitting around Isabelle's bassinet sipping from their teacups, especially seeing as the baby couldn't hold her own cup, requiring Clara to do it for her instead.

"Ahh, nothing like a drop of Earl Grey to get you through an afternoon slump, I always say," said Isabelle, smacking her lips upon draining her cup.

The children had certainly never heard her say this before — of this, they were certain — nor had they ever known her to have a drop of tea in all her life.

"Listen, you must be feeling very tired," said Everett. "Why don't we put you down for a nap."

"I beg your pardon!" said Isabelle in outrage. "I won't be disposed of so quickly! Now that I'm finally getting some attention around here, there are a few things I'd like you to do for me. For starters, you can cut me in on all that money you've got over there."

"But you can't even spend it!" said Clara.

Isabelle pursed her lips. "Silly girl. Haven't you ever heard of trust funds?"

All three children shook their heads.

"Now listen, I know about these things," began the baby.

"But that's just it," Charles interrupted, "we don't see how! We've had to go to school and everything to learn things."

"Have you now? Aw, well, you must be quite slow."

She then insisted they dole out the money evenly in piles before them like dealing a deck of cards — one pile for Clara, one for Charles, another for Everett, and another yet for herself, and she surveyed the whole process to make sure they didn't cheat her. She was just about to insist they count her share for her when there was suddenly a knock upon the back door.

The children turned to see the freckled face of Jimmy Holbrook peering through the glass.

"You've got to come see!" he yelled excitedly once Everett answered the door. "My aunt's dog just had puppies! Ten of them!"

Clara jumped to her feet. "Puppies! Oh, let's go! I want to see!"

"Uh, but what about ... ?" Charles inclined his head in the baby's direction rather than finish the sentence.

"We'll only be gone a minute," replied Everett. "She can't go anywhere. Come on then!"

The three children yanked on their shoes and had almost closed the door behind them when baby Isabelle shouted, "Where do you think you're going?!"

Jimmy's jaw dropped open. "Was that—?"

"*No!*" said Everett, Charles, and Clara together, hurrying away from the house.

"But I could have sworn I—"

"You didn't," said Everett. "What kind of puppies did you say they were?" he asked in an attempt to change the subject.

"I didn't say," Jimmy reluctantly answered. "They're collies, I think." And collies they were, though you couldn't tell by looking, for their pink skin was merely fuzzy, and their little eyes had yet to open.

It might have only been a short visit had it not been for Jimmy's aunt. She'd wanted to know all about Clara and where she was from, and then she'd inquired about Father and Watson and whether they'd found work, and the children could only say so little and appear so rushed without seeming rude.

By the time they managed to drag Clara away from the puppies and rush back to the house, nearly ten minutes had passed, and they opened the door to find a horrific scene unfolding. The puppies now seemed such a foolhardy distraction. Watson was in the kitchen flopped upon a stool, wiping his forehead and blinking profusely as if trying to snap out of a trance.

"Wha' wha' — wha's happening to me?! She's been speakin'! She couldn't speak before ... c-could she? Oh, I must be going mad. My Uncle Ulysses went mad, you know. Oh, it'll be the looney bin for me now. Been talking to me about her finances, she has! Says she's struck it rich! Then she said ... oh, but I m-must be dreaming. That's what it is!"

"Of course you're only dreaming," said Everett, quickly running to Watson's side. "All you need is a good rest, and this will all be forgotten. Come — we'll take you up to your room."

Clara reached out to grab Watson by the hand. "It's okay Mr. Watson, sir, you're not going mad. It's this heat. We've all been feeling sort of funny. Be a dear and take a nap. That's a love," she added kindly as he followed them up the stairs to his room in a daze.

They ran back down the stairs a moment later to find baby Isabelle spouting something about Watson having gone "crackers", though she threw in a bunch of psychiatric terminology they'd never heard before.

"Quick, let's get that diaper off before anyone else hears her!" said Everett.

"Don't you dare!" Isabelle fumed, pounding her tiny fists upon the rail of her bassinet. "I'll scream!"

"No one will be expecting *you* to scream, and by the time they hear you we'll have the turban off and you'll be back to whining and babbling," said Everett, coldly.

"No, don't! *Please*! Have I told you what sweet little children you are? Don't take the turban off — it's pure silk! Fit for a queen! Not like those itchy cloth diapers Mother puts on me."

Clara was beginning to feel guilty, and was overcome by her powers of empathy. "We're sorry, that must be awful!" she cried.

"It is," said the baby, now pouting as pathetically as possible.

"Don't listen to her, Clara," Everett barked. "We can't let anyone else hear her talking — we must get that turban off!" he said, and then turned to his brother. "Charles — you get the money up off the floor before Mother sees it!"

And so, with a kicking and screaming and flailing of porky little limbs, Everett and Clara finally had the turban in hand, and a moment later when Mother came running down the stairs, baby Isabelle was back in her bassinet with a squinched up face, wailing her little head off.

"Good heavens, Isabelle, whatever's the matter?" said Mother, rushing to the bassinet.

But baby Isabelle could no longer say, and the children were quite sure she shot them a very dirty look as Mother picked her up and patted her on the back, humming softly to sooth her.

Mother laughed. "You know, it was the strangest thing," she told the children. "I was up in my sewing room and I could have sworn I heard a *woman* crying!

But when I got down here, it was only little baby Isabelle ... oh, how the mind plays tricks!"

The children heaved a collective sigh of relief, and were further grateful when Watson came down the stairs for dinner shortly after complaining of bizarre dreams and nothing more. It all seemed really rather funny upon reflection, but nonetheless they were careful never to let the turban anywhere near baby Isabelle again.

"You know, I've been thinking," said Clara afterward. "Perhaps the reason babies don't talk until they're older is because they have to learn to be polite first."

And Charles and Everett both agreed that this was the second-wisest thing she'd said yet.

In Which Everett Runs A Taxi Service

After such nearly disastrous encounters with a gypsy, a mob of angry gamblers, and an overly loquacious baby, the children might have been wise to place the turban safely back in its trunk. Surely this would have been the sensible thing to do, but then again, such things as sense and sensibility rarely make for good books (though one exception does come to mind). Therefore, as the one telling you this story, it was lucky for me that Everett, Charles and Clara weren't at all sensible when it came to magical objects, and they were soon fighting over who would get to take their turn with the turban next — a dispute which Everett quickly won for he was easily the meanest.

I should warn you that this adventure is a particularly long one in the telling. I tried to get the characters to summarize and use their words sparingly, but there was so very much that they wanted to include, and we all know how Everett can be when you try to reason with him. Therefore, I'll do my best to tell it to you in smaller bits so you don't grow overtired, and because I know how nice it is to have a tidy little spot here and there to place your bookmark when you start to feel sleepy or your mother calls you for supper.

This adventure begins the day after the previous one. The children were once again trudging up the hill toward the old motorcar, the turban tucked under Everett's arm, when they spotted The Man with the Very Large Mustache Indeed with his head stuck under the hood of the car. He was whistling through the gap in his teeth and twisting a wrench around a rusty bolt with his grease-stained hands.

The children were about to greet him when he stood up, wiped his forehead with an equally greasy handkerchief, and then slammed the hood of the car shut with a terrific thud.

"Ah," he said at the sight of them. "Perfect timing. She's all fixed up!"

"All fixed up?" repeated Everett. "What for?"

"Found a buyer — a collector of sorts from Philadelphia. He's coming down in a few weeks to make the purchase, so I'm afraid you children won't be able to play in the car anymore. It's too dangerous with it being fully functional again and all. Sorry about that," he grunted, reaching down to grab up his tools.

"That's awfully sad," said Charles, woefully, "but I suppose you needed the money."

"It doesn't hurt," replied the man, his lips barely visible beneath the peppery spans of mustache for which he was named.

"Could we at least sit in it one last time?" asked Clara.

The man considered this. "Shucks, why not. Just don't go touching anything," he said. He then limped away in the direction of his house, his knees looking as though they might soon buckle under the weight of his tool box.

The children hopped into the car and ran their hands lovingly along the red leather seats. Everett hadn't said a word since hearing that their car was to be sold, and his poor little face looked like that of a sea captain's who'd just watched his boat sink.

"Perhaps the buyer will change his mind," said Clara comfortingly, "or get stuck in a snow storm on his way down."

"In the middle of June?" snapped Charles.

"Oh, I suppose not — I was only trying to help."

Everett fingered the steering wheel. "It's probably for the best. We were getting a bit old for all these pretend games anyway," he said finally.

"That's the saddest thing I've ever heard," said Charles. "I bet Peter Pan would never say anything so dreadful."

"Peter Pan's made up!" Everett shot back.

"What?!" cried Clara.

"Oh, never mind that," said Everett. "The man with the mustache isn't the only one who needs money. There's got to be some talent the turban can grant me that'll help us to make some."

"What sort of talent would you like?" asked Clara.

"I haven't thought of one just yet," he said.

"Perhaps it's not a talent turban at all," said Charles thoughtfully. "Perhaps it's a wishing turban and all we have to do is *ask* it for the money. Go on — ask it for a penny and see what happens."

Everett looked as though he'd have liked very much to say how childish such an idea was, but was too curious himself to refuse, and so he held the turban out in front of him and stated very clearly "We require a penny."

"No, no, no," said Charles. "I've read about this in books. You have to say 'I wish'."

Everett tried again. "*I wish* for a penny," he said.

"What was that?!" cried Clara as something landed upon the dashboard.

"It's only a beetle," said Everett.

"Are you sure?" she asked. "It looks coppery."

Everett was about to shout something about knowing very well the difference between a beetle and a penny, but then the object flew away and saved him the trouble.

"I suppose it's not a wishing turban after all," said Charles.

"No, I think not," agreed Everett. "Back to needing a talent."

"Put the turban on and maybe something will come to you," Clara suggested.

For lack of a better idea, Everett obliged and sat the turban atop his head, quite surprised by the tingling feeling that shot down his spine as he did so.

"What's happened?" asked Charles, spotting the goofy look upon his brother's face.

Everett would have been hard pressed to explain. He suddenly felt very sure of himself, as though he could do anything he pleased — climb the tallest tree, solve the trickiest math problem, build a car from scratch ... or even *drive*!

"I'm going to drive," he said decidedly.

"What? But you can't!" cried Charles and Clara in unison.

"Sure I can," said Everett. "I just feel it's what I'm *supposed* to do, you know?"

Charles and Clara didn't. "You don't mean to drive *this* car do you?" said Charles worriedly.

"Of course!" sang Everett. It was as though the turban had taken over all his senses. "Lucky it was just fixed, right?"

"But the man with the mustache said we weren't to touch anything!" Charles insisted.

"He only said that because he thinks we don't know how to drive! But now I *do* know how to drive — go on, ask me what this thing does," he said, pointing to a long stick with a handle on the end of it, and when Charles did so, Everett replied so knowledgeably that both Charles and Clara doubted Henry Ford himself could have given a better answer.

"What if the mustached man sees that the car is missing?" said Clara. "We could go to prison for stealing!"

"He can't see the car from his house," Everett protested. "Plus, he works during the day, so he shan't be home!"

Everett hopped from the car.

"Where are you going?" the others shouted.

"I need to get a few things from the house," he replied, and with no further explanation, he trod down the hill and out of sight with the turban still atop his head.

Charles and Clara hurried after him. "What sort of things?" they asked.

"Well, I can't very well drive people around town looking like this, can I?" he called over his shoulder. "Wait here," he told them before disappearing through the back door of the house.

Exasperated, Charles and Clara pondered all the sorts of trouble they could get into as they waited for Everett to reappear, and when he returned moments later, he was wearing one of Father's dinner jackets, a pair of shiny black shoes that were much too large for him, and a timepiece dangling from his pocket. In his hands was a furry looking object which Charles soon recognized as the beard from a Santa costume, and he had a bowler-rimmed hat wedged beneath his arm.

"How do I look?" he asked them.

"Like a very, very little man," sighed Clara.

Everett scowled. "There *are* some men my size, you know."

Charles was going to say something about the munchkins from *The Wonderful Wizard Of Oz*, but thought better of it.

"So, I've been thinking," Everett began. "You two better stay behind — you can keep watch for The Man with the Very Large Mustache Indeed — it would look awfully funny having two children in the car with me, anyway."

Charles and Clara stared blankly at him as he placed the bowler hat down overtop the turban on his head.

"We can't let you go alone. What if something happens?!" cried Charles.

"Nothing's going to happen! I've driven cars loads of times," said Everett with a confidant air.

"No you haven't," said Charles. "You only *think* you've done!"

"It's that turban," said Clara hopelessly. "Baby Isabelle thought all sorts of things she'd never thought before while she was wearing it too."

Everett was unfazed by their pleas and marched purposefully (albeit a bit clumsily in his father's shoes) back up the hill toward the old motorcar with the other two in tow, both reasoning with him every step of the way.

"I'll be back by dinner, and hopefully with some money," he told them as he rounded the front of the car and yanked upon the hand crank. When the engine purred to life as it had never done before, Everett gave a satisfied smile, and then perched himself behind the wheel with his chest puffed out and nose held high. He had only to put on a pair of driving goggles, which he'd snatched from the pocket of Father's car coat, and shift the car into gear before he was off, motoring down the hill and waving to Charles and Clara over his shoulder, their last feeble protests drowned out by the roaring of the engine.

"Oh, heavens! What are we to do?!" cried Clara as the car sputtered away and out of sight.

Charles hadn't an answer for this. The lingering exhaust fumes that filled his lungs stank of betrayal, and he felt a tightening sensation in the middle of his chest. Of all the times he'd been angry with his brother, this was by far the angriest. Everett may have belittled him and called him names or made him feel small and cowardly at times, but he'd never before run off without him.

The two children flopped helplessly upon the ground, brewing silently in the hot summer sun with only an occasional heavy sigh for conversation.

When words were again exchanged, it was Clara who said, "It would serve cousin Everett right if we never spoke another word to him."

Charles did not immediately respond. Though he quite agreed, he was feeling especially ill-tempered about this new involuntary alliance with Clara. He supposed this should make him feel more sympathetic toward his cousin, seeing as he and Everett had teamed up against her plenty of times, but he wasn't feeling especially kind-hearted at the moment.

"Do you think we ought to wait here until he comes back?" asked Clara.

"Probably," mumbled Charles. "Mother would wonder if we came back to the house without him."

The hours crept by as they awaited Everett's return, lying on their backs and yanking blade after blade of grass from the earth, and playing game after game of tic tack toe and hangman in a patch of dirt. When they finally heard the tell-tale rumble of the motorcar climbing back up the hill, it was nearly dinnertime, and Charles and Clara were particularly hungry for they hadn't dared go back to the house for a snack lest Mother should barrage them with questions. Their hunger did nothing to resolve their anger, and they folded their arms across their chests and stared petulantly at Everett as he steered the car onto the spot it had always sat, shifted the gear, and hopped out, all the while smiling and jingling a pocket full of coins.

"Aw, come on now," he said upon seeing their faces. "You two can't still be mad, can you?"

Charles and Clara bristled, but uttered not a word.

"Oh, let's call a truce," said Everett. "I do so want to tell you what's happened, and I know you want to hear."

After a whispered debate of presidential proportions, Charles finally turned to Everett and said, "Okay, truce. But only while you're telling us. Then we reserve the right to reinstate the silent treatment."

"Fine," said Everett. He then proceeded to tell them all about a gentleman selling encyclopedia door to door who was so overcome by the heat that he gladly paid Everett a penny for each door he drove him to, and then ten percent of his commission on each set of encyclopedia he sold. "And he sold four sets in three hours," continued Everett. "Look at all this money I made!" He held out his jacket pocket so they could peer in at the mass of copper and silver coins.

"Gee willikers!" cried Charles, so impressed that he felt his anger quickly slipping away. "Well, I suppose we can hardly stay mad at you when you've made so much money for Mother and Father ... but you've had your turn with the turban now, and tomorrow we'll do something much less dangerous."

"Oh, no!" Everett declared. "We're not giving up the chance to make this sort of money again. I figure I'll start my own taxi company."

"No you won't!" said Clara in such a tone of authority that both Everett and Charles were taken by surprise. "It's not fair — you get all the fun, and we've nothing better to do than pull up grass."

"Fine then," said Everett. "You'll come with me. I'll need your help anyways."

This was not the answer Charles and Clara had been expecting. They'd gotten themselves all ready to argue the dangerousness of Everett's driving a car, but now that they were included, it sounded altogether less precarious.

"But what will people think of two children riding in the car with you?" asked Clara.

Everett furrowed his brow in thought. "We'll dress you up," he said decisively. "That way only one of you is a child. You can be Charles's grandmother who's shrunken to a very small height with age."

"Oh! What fun!" cried Clara, happily. "I love dress-up games!"

Charles, on the other hand, did not look especially pleased at the idea of being a doted upon grandson with lollipop and beanie, but he preferred that to playing hangman in the dirt all day again with Clara.

Having settled upon the next day's events, and with all anger forgotten, Everett left his costume in the car, and they walked home to their supper. Mother had fixed leg of lamb, wild rice and asparagus, and Clara ate almost all of her asparagus without one mention of Cook's superior method of preparation. Then, when they had all quite finished, the three children ran up the stairs to discuss the details of Everett's taxi business in private.

"We'll be needing some sort of advertisements," said Charles once the nursery door had been shut behind them.

"That's what I've been thinking," said Everett. "We'll use Father's typewriter to make up some flyers."

"We could put them in people's mailboxes," Clara suggested.

"No," said Everett. "That'll take much too long. I have an idea, but it might take some thinking ... Jimmy Holbrook's elder brother, Peter, runs the local paper route ... if we could only mange to slip our flyers into the newspapers before he delivers them ..."

"That's brilliant," said Charles.

"Yes, but I haven't figured out how we're supposed to do that without his knowing," said Everett, and when Charles and Clara continued to stare blankly back at him, he added, "We can't tell him what we're doing! He knows I'm not old enough to drive."

"Oh, I see," said Charles, and Clara pretended as though she did. "What if one of us were to distract him while another put the flyers inside the papers?" he said.

"Hmm," thought Everett. "I like it," he said, and after further thought, he'd devised a plan. "Clara — you'll ask Peter to show you his aunt's puppies. If we catch him at the right time, he'll have his bicycle out with the little basket on front for the papers, and while you're gone, I'll sneak out from behind a bush and slip the flyers inside."

The children felt better having a plan, and were then occupied with the task of typing up a flyer and deciding exactly what it should say. A great deal of argument was to be had over the naming of the taxi company. Everett wanted to call it "The Lightning Taxi Service", but Charles said "Oh, no," and Clara said "Oh, no indeed," and they both insisted that the word "lightning" was much too suggestive of bad weather, and or driving at such fast speeds that passengers might go tumbling right out the back of the car. In the end they decided upon the name "The Coopstown Taxi Company", which was at least practical if not exciting.

"I'll go and get the typewriter from under Mother and Father's bed — you two keep watch," said Everett.

Charles and Clara waited as innocently as possible in the hallway, but neither Father, Mother, nor Watson passed through, and a moment later Everett returned lugging a heavy black box and several sheets of paper.

The nursery door was shut behind them once more, and the box was opened upon the floor, the silver latches clicking free to reveal Father's shiny black typewriter.

"Un-der-wood," said Charles, reading the name stamped above the keytop. "What do you suppose that means?"

"I think it's German for 'typewriter'," said Everett, knowledgeably.

"Shouldn't there be a little umlaut over the 'u' then?"

"Oh, how should I know?" replied Everett, irritably. "I only said I *thought* it was German." He grabbed for a sheet of paper and slipped it behind the platen (which is the rolly thing that spins the paper about as you type).

"Do you know how to use one of these?" asked Clara.

"Of course I know how to use one of these," said Everett. "I've watched Father do it loads of times. You just press the buttons with the letters you want, and then you hit this long black key here to put spaces between the words," Everett explained, pointing to the space bar. He then began to type the name "Coopstown Taxi Company", the typewriter clicking and clanking a lot more loudly than he'd have liked considering there wasn't usually an awful lot of clicking and clanking coming from the nursery.

When each of the letters of the company name had been typed upon the page, the three children sat back to contemplate the look of them.

"I suppose it looks alright," said Everett.

"I'm not so sure ..." began Charles. "Some of the letters look a bit wonky," he said.

"Maybe some of them should be capitalled," suggested Clara.

"That's capital*ized*," Charles corrected, "... or is it capital*icensed*?" he wondered, second guessing himself. One can never be too sure of these things.

"It doesn't matter — I don't know how to type the big letters anyway, so we'll just have to keep the little ones," said Everett, and he began to type again, *click click click*, and even more clicks, and another *click click*, and then there was a loud *ding* like a kitchen timer, and the children leapt back in surprise.

"That can't be good," said Clara, fretfully.

"*Wait* — I think the same thing happened to Father once, and he gave this little lever here a push," said Everett, sliding a metal bar to the right until there was another ding. "There. I think that's done it," he said, and he typed a few more words before coming to a stop. "Hold on ... how are the customers supposed to tell us when they want rides?"

This stumped Charles and Clara as well, but Everett's face soon lit up with an idea.

"I know — we'll use the telephone in Father's shop!"

Charles looked queasy at the thought. "But mightn't we get in trouble?"

"Oh, don't be chicken," said Everett. "Nobody goes in there anymore since it burned down. Now if we only knew the phone number."

"It's Coopstown fifty-two B thirteen," said Clara, matter-of-factly.

Both Charles and Everett appraised her curiously. "How could you possibly know that?" said Everett.

"Because that's what my mum tells the lady on the other end of the telephone whenever she calls Auntie Mary," she replied.

"Hmm," hummed Everett, suspiciously. "You're sure?"

"Positive," said Clara with a nod.

"Well, alright, but you better not be mistaken," he said, and he typed the letters and numbers onto the page, heaving a sigh of accomplishment when he'd finished. "There — that'll do quite nicely."

Charles and Clara peered over his shoulder at the completed advertisement, which read:

```
coopstown taxi company. we take you where you want
   to go for 10 cents. telephone coopstown 52b13.
```

"It's very good," said Clara, and with that agreed upon, Everett set about typing the advertisement several more times down the page and then quite a few extra times down another, occasionally rubbing the paper with a little round eraser they'd found at the bottom of the box when he struck the wrong key by mistake. It was quite an easy thing to do, for typewriters were tricky things and you had to hit the keys in just the right places or you ended up with inky letters where you didn't want them.

When all the typing was finished and the typewriter had been placed back in its box and returned to its home beneath Mother and Father's bed, they found a pair of scissors in the drawer where they kept the paints and coloring paper, and Clara offered to cut the advertisements into little slips because she was good at cutting in a straight line.

"Good work, boys," said Everett once all the little slips of paper were stacked neatly in a pile and the scissors had been returned to their drawer.

Clara might have argued that she was very much a girl, and perhaps she should have, but she knew that coming from her cousin, this was high praise indeed.

Mother had learned not to question the children dashing off so quickly after breakfast any more, and the next morning they were out the door even earlier than usual seeing as they wanted to catch Peter Holbrook before he began his paper route.

The grass was still ripe with morning dew and the sun glowed low upon the horizon as they stepped outside.

"Now remember," said Everett, "ask about seeing the puppies, and if he says no ... well, let's just hope he doesn't."

As expected, Peter was by his bicycle when they arrived to the Holbrook residence, and Everett ducked behind a bush before he could be spotted, which left Charles and Clara standing awkwardly in the middle of the road.

Clara was fidgeting nervously because it felt like such a sneaky plan even though she *did* really want to see the puppies.

"Hi!" said Peter when he noticed the two children idling outside his house.

"Hello, Peter," said Charles. "We've, um, come to inquire about the puppies."

"Oh! Did you want to buy one?" asked Peter. He was just placing a bundle of newspapers into his bike basket.

"No!" Charles quickly replied. "Poncho would probably eat it! We — well, Jimmy showed them to us the other day, but they'd just been born and their eyes hadn't even opened yet, so we just thought we might like to see them again."

"Oh, I see," said Peter genially. "Well, I have to be off to deliver these papers, but I can show you later if you like — Jimmy may even be out of bed by then."

"Well," said Charles, which was all he could think of to say at first, "we only want a quick look, you see ... Clara had a nightmare — yes, a nightmare about the puppies. She dreamt that they all went missing," he said, implicating his cousin. "So we just thought we'd check to make sure they hadn't. She'd feel so much better, wouldn't you, Clara?"

The girl gulped and then nodded.

"It was a very life-like dream, wasn't it, Clara?"

She nodded once more.

Peter looked worried. "I hope it wasn't a psychic dream! Aunt Mildred gets those. She once dreamt her husband was attacked by a killer cow, and the next day he got run over by the milk truck!"

Charles very much hoped that the puppies were not missing at all, or else he should feel very guilty for making up such a morbid story. He and Clara were taken next door to Peter's aunt's house to check on the puppies, and they were all three relieved to find them exactly where they were supposed to be. Clara said how darling they looked with their little blue eyes, and Peter let her hold one for a minute seeing as she'd been so worried, or so Charles had said, and then a few minutes later they were waving goodbye to Peter as he rode off on his bicycle. They'd nearly forgotten about Everett when he popped out at them from behind a bush.

"I've done it!" he said cheerfully.

"That's wonderful!" said Clara. "And the puppies weren't missing after all!"

"They weren't *ever* missing," Charles reminded her.

"Oh, right," she said. "I was beginning to remember *having* that dream — it was awfully clever of you, Charles, even if it was a lie."

"It wasn't the *bad* sort of lie in which people get hurt or cover up very dark secrets," said Charles defensively, and he explained to Everett all about the story he'd made up so that Peter would take them to see the puppies.

"Quick thinking, mate," said Everett, and Charles beamed.

"So what are we to do next?" asked Clara.

"We wait," Everett replied. "We'll tell Mother we're out playing, but we'll really be inside Father's stock room in case the telephone rings."

This sounded like a good plan, but the children quickly discovered that stockrooms can be very dull places, especially ones connected to burned down grocery stores. There were boxes and crates full of canned goods and rotting vegetables which the children sat upon as they stared anxiously up at the telephone on the wall.

"We should start getting calls very soon," Everett assured them. "People will be wanting rides to their luncheons and afternoon appointments."

This thought contented the children for quite some time, and they amused themselves with guessing games involving the contents of each crate and container, but still the phone did not ring.

"I had hoped we might have received at least one call by now," said Everett, feeling as though he'd waited a very grown-up amount of time before becoming impatient.

They were all so eager for the telephone to ring that every noise they heard began to sound like ringing. Once, Clara thought Charles's sneeze was an incoming call, and then later the squeak of a mouse somewhere in the corner sent all the children scrambling for the telephone.

"Oh, what's the use! It may never ring," said Charles in frustration. "And I'm getting awfully hungry." Charles was very attentive to his meal times, even when helping to run a taxi business. "People probably suspect we're at lunch and they're just being polite by not calling, so let's go have a bit of something and perhaps we'll have better luck when we get back."

Everett felt sure that the second they left, the phone would start to ring, but he too was quite hungry. "Well, alright — but let's be quick!"

With their minds set upon eating, they were about to slip inside the house when there suddenly came a jingling from the telephone on the wall. They were quite sure it was the telephone this time, and the children fell over one another in a frenzy to answer it.

Everett pulled himself out from underneath Clara and was the first to reach the phone.

"Coopstown Fellytone Company," he shouted into the receiver. "I mean —— Coopstown *Telephone* Company."

"You mean *taxi* company," Clara hissed.

"Right — Taxi's Coopstown Company," he said once more, but sensing he'd gotten it wrong again, he sighed. "Oh, bother! How can we help you?"

"Marjorie Whimpole calling, dear," said a voice with a low warble. "I require your services for this afternoon. Your advertisement couldn't have come at a better time. There's the Ladies Auxiliary in a couple of hours and I can't walk great distances in this heat. Besides, I've bad hips."

"We're at your service, madam," said Everett, trying to sound like the sort of professional that goes about answering telephones all day. "When and where shall the driver pick you up?"

"About a quarter till three at 9532 Bauer Avenue — It's just across from the tea shop on Elm — you know of it, I'm sure?"

"Oh, yes, of course," said Everett, which wasn't true, but he knew once the turban was atop his head he'd know just where to go.

"Listen, at these prices, and in this heat, I'm sure the whole of the Ladies Auxiliary will want rides. Shall I supply you with all their names and addresses?"

Everett fumbled for words. "Erm—"

"On second thought, why go to the trouble! Just pick me up and I'll direct you to each of their houses. I'm very good with directions, you know — I was with Air Traffic Control during the war."

"Were you really?" said Everett, for he quite liked planes.

"I was indeed," bellowed the woman. (In truth, I couldn't find any evidence of a lady air traffic controller

127

during WWI, but Mrs. Whimpole was very insistent). "Well then — I'll expect a driver at a quarter till three. Good day to you," she said.

Everett placed the receiver back on its hook. "We've just been hired to drive the whole of the Ladies Artillery!" he told Charles and Clara.

"What's that?" said Clara.

"I've no idea," said Everett. "I suspect they collect guns and cannons and things."

"Perhaps they put on Civil War reenactments," said Charles.

"Maybe so," said Everett. "Anyway, we're sure to make loads of money. There must be quite a lot of ladies in an artillery."

With the acquisition of their very first customer, the children had their lunch. I won't bore you with the details as I'm sure you don't care to hear that they had ham and cheese sandwiches, or that Charles spilled his milk on the floor and was aided in the cleaning up by Mother and Poncho. I'll also spare you the details of the children's rummaging about in the attic in search of a costume for Clara, for attics are very dirty, dusty places, and several nasty spiders were encountered on this particular occasion.

Things didn't get interesting again for the Swope children (*and* Clara, who was not technically a Swope) until the middle of the afternoon when it had come time for Everett to pick up Mrs. Whimpole.

Charles and Clara seated themselves in the front seat of the old motorcar next to Everett so as to leave room for customers in the back.

"Now we're not to act as though we know one another," said Everett once he'd started the engine.

"Right," Clara said, adjusting her hat — a musty old thing with several decorative plums dangling off the end of it. Luckily, Grandma Swope had left several trunks full of clothes to Mother after she'd died, and Clara was now looking sufficiently aged in a wool skirt and a lace collared blouse. To complete the look, they'd then stuffed her with several pillows and made her hair white with face powder, all of which Clara loved because dress-up games were her favorite.

Charles was looking as he always did, and Everett was once again clad in Father's old jacket, shoes, bowler hat, and of course the Santa beard and turban.

Squeezed in between the two of them, Charles made himself as small as possible. "Good grief! You two look crackers!"

"Charles, popkin, mind your manners," said Clara, giving her tiny charge a peck on the cheek and wiping away the resulting lipstick smear with a licked finger.

"*Ew*, gross," whined Charles. "Can we get on with it already?" he said testily, scowling up at Clara who was delighting in her grandmotherly role.

"Hold onto your hats — it's going to be a bumpy ride!" sang Everett, and the motorcar thundered down the hill and into town, Everett honking and waving happily to the townspeople on foot.

Folks smiled and waved back at them as they passed by, for in 1920 people were still often cheered by the sight of a shiny motorcar upon the road.

Guided by the knowledge bestowed upon him by the turban, Everett found the tea shop on the corner of Elm Street straight away, and directly across from it was a stately brick home with a lively garden the likes of which brings many a retired person joy and satisfaction in their dotage.

"This must be it!" said Everett, pulling up in front of the house.

Mrs. Whimpole must have been watching for the car at her window, because not a moment later a very sturdy looking woman with a straw hat and a walking stick barreled purposefully out the front door.

Everett hopped out to lend a hand.

"No!" she said when he reached for her walking stick. "I don't need any assistance — just fetch the door, will you?" She appraised Everett with beady eyes, clearly thinking what a tiny man he was, especially since she was twice the size of him herself.

The car tilted to one side as she pulled herself into the back seat, refilling her strained lungs with very deep breaths.

Charles and Clara thought she looked a bit old to be in an artillery, and they'd half expected her to have a rifle slung over her shoulder, but instead she was merely clutching a leather bound day planner to her chest.

"Ah, who do we have here?" she said upon spotting Charles and Clara in the front seat. "I do hope you're not running behind in your appointments! I pride myself on punctuality."

"Don't worry Missus Whimpole," said Everett, trying to sound very manly. "I'll drop you and the other ladies off first. These two are going to the ... uh, to the port!"

"Are they? I just love steamboats! Though I much prefer planes," she said, shoving her hand out in front of Clara to be shaken. "Marjorie Whimpole — retired Air Traffic Control."

"Pleased to meet you," said Clara weakly. "I'm ... Greta. Yes, Greta, uh, Tulips," Clara added, having come up with the name just then as she peered into the woman's garden. "And this is my grandson, Charles."

"Charmed, I'm sure. And where are you two off to?" she asked them. Everett meanwhile steered the car back onto the road ("Take the next left!" he was ordered).

"Uh," thought Clara, "England — London!"

"Good gracious, are you really? I thought the Old Bay Line only went to Virginia! Added a transatlantic service, have they?" asked Mrs. Whimpole. However, much to the children's relief, she was quickly distracted and didn't require an answer. "Third house on the right," she barked at Everett, and he soon pulled the car up in front of another house with an equally colorful garden.

"This'll be Missus Brown — can't stand the woman, but her husband's in oil or something. Anyway — she gives a lot of money."

A tiny woman with boney features and a pill box hat alighted from the house and was helped into the back of the car alongside Mrs. Whimpole by Everett.

"Betty, darling — how wonderful to see you," gushed Mrs. Whimpole, offering Mrs. Brown a firm embrace as though she were being paid to do it.

The woman returned the greeting in a delicate voice but was not allowed another two words before Mrs. Whimpole began directing Everett to another house a few blocks away.

Charles and Clara marveled at Everett's driving ability, especially how he avoided all the mailboxes and buildings, and he never hit any cats or squirrels either.

"This is Missus Tulips and her grandson, Charles," Mrs. Whimpole told Mrs. Brown.

"How nice," said Mrs. Brown, giving Clara's hand a shake with a feather light grip. "Will you be joining the Ladies Auxiliary, Missus Tulips?" she added.

"Why, what a splendid idea — I should have thought of it myself," said Mrs. Whimpole. "They're off to London just now," she told Mrs. Brown, "but that's no matter — we meet every Wednesday!"

Clara fumbled for words. "Em — I can't!" she stammered.

"Why the devil not?" said Mrs. Whimpole.

"Well ... I don't much like guns, you see ... and I'm very old — I can barely get up and down the stairs anymore. I'm eighty-seven after all."

"Good heavens!" said Mrs. Whimpole, and both ladies were clutching their chests. "Why, your skin's as smooth as a baby's bottom — whatever's your secret?"

Charles and Everett both stifled a laugh, and Clara elbowed her alleged grandson angrily in the side.

"Well ... it's simple really," Clara began, hoping she'd be able to finish. "Um ... banana peels!"

"*Banana* peels?" recited the women incredulously.

"Yes," said Clara, now feeling quite clever. "It's all the rage in England right now. That's why His Majesty was looking so young in the papers last week."

"Now that you mention it, Greta, that Churchill fellow was looking handsomer as well ..." said Mrs. Whimpole.

"And you just rub them over your face, do you?" asked Mrs. Brown.

"Just before bed," answered Clara.

"Why you and I should try it, Betty," said Mrs. Whimpole. "You could use some help with those dreadful frown lines, dear."

"And *you* with your crow's feet," said Mrs. Brown tartly.

They were spared any additional nitpicking, for just then Everett was helping another lady into the car, this time a Mrs. Gatsby who was much younger and wearing far too much makeup.

"Darling!" she said in greeting Mrs. Whimpole, and another "Darling!" in greeting Mrs. Brown, and there were fake kisses blown, though none were reciprocated.

Everett was directed to the next house, and upon the journey Mrs. Whimpole told Mrs. Gatsby all about banana peels and their cure for wrinkles, and she insisted on Clara turning around so that Mrs. Gatsby could see just what banana peels could do for eighty-year-old skin, only Clara tried not to lean in too close should any of the ladies see through her clever disguise.

"Amazing, darling — simply amazing!" Gushed Mrs. Gatsby. "Of course, I'm much too young for wrinkles myself ..."

"Um," said Everett, interrupting. "Where are we to put the next two passengers?" He'd pulled the car up in front of a pale blue house where two elderly ladies with matching wicker handbags were waiting by the side of the road.

"Oh, the Randall sisters," said Mrs. Whimpole. "Yes, they're the last to be picked up."

Clara saw a simple solution to the problem. "Come now, Charles dear," she said, grabbing for Charles's hand. "Let's you and I get in the rumble seat to make room for these nice ladies." She hopped from the car with great agility and aided Charles in doing the same.

Mrs. Whimpole looked startled. "But mightn't you—"

"Surely one of us could—" began Mrs. Brown.

"Darling! Do be careful," said Mrs. Gatsby.

But by the time Clara remembered that eighty-year-olds were not usually so sprightly on their feet, she'd already slung her leg over the side of the rumble seat and hopped in, pulling Charles up alongside her by the arm.

The whole of the Ladies Auxiliary (or Artillery, depending on who you ask) was staring wide-eyed at Clara with their jaws unhinged in a most unbecoming and impolite manner, and each of the ladies' faces were still that way when Everett unloaded them from the car outside the town hall a few minutes later.

Once the three children were finally alone, Everett turned on Clara. "Since when do eighty-seven-year-old grannies ride in rumble seats?!" he snapped. "Greta Tulips, indeed! I wish I *was* dropping you off at the port."

"I'm sorry — I wasn't thinking! We'd all gotten so chummy over the banana peels that I forgot myself for a moment," she said, her eyes filling with tears.

"Hmm," growled Everett, reproachfully. "Well at least we made some money, and there's more to come because they'll all be wanting rides home in an hour — but you're not to go doing any jumping jacks or cartwheels! Understood?"

This was agreed upon, and over the next hour Clara took the liberty of developing a deathly sounding cough and a hand tremor, so that by the time the ladies returned from their meeting, they were quickly concerned and all over Clara with offerings of throat lozenges and unused hankies.

"Poor dear," said Mrs. Whimpole. "But whatever happened to your ship? Aren't you supposed to be on your way to London?"

The children had quite forgotten about this part of the story.

"They've just got back," said Everett quickly.

Clara nodded (and coughed). "It was only for lunch."

All five ladies burst into fits of laughter. "Darling, you're a riot!" guffawed Mrs. Gatsby, and the two sisters giggled girlishly while Mrs. Whimpole chortled and said, "Impossible! You wouldn't even be halfway across the Atlantic yet!"

The children were feeling very squeamish, and decided the only sensible thing to do was to laugh along.

135

"Tell us, darling, what d'ya have for lunch?" cried Mrs. Gatsby in mirth, and the peals of laughter began anew.

The Mrs. Randalls and Mrs. Gatsby were soon deposited in front of their houses, and then it was just Mrs. Brown and Mrs. Whimpole left in the car, both of whom were now discussing items for the upcoming bake sale and arguing over who should play the lead in the amateur operetta. Charles was quite disappointed that not one word was spoken of Civil War reenactments, and as for Everett, he wasn't paying any attention at all because the heat had made his face all itchy under the beard and he was busy scratching his neck and cheeks. He had just turned the car onto Mrs. Brown's street and was having a scratch around the ears when suddenly a gust of wind snatched the Santa beard right off his face and sent it flying through the air to be consumed by the cloud of dust trailing behind the car.

Everett hadn't time to react before one of the ladies spotted his clean-shaven face and did a double-take.

"Didn't you have a beard earlier?" said Mrs. Brown. "Marjorie — tell me I haven't lost my marbles — he had a beard earlier! All white and fluffy!"

"I say," Mrs. Whimpole very much said, "he did indeed! Whatever's happened to it?" she demanded.

"Um ... it fell off," said Everett, though he instantly regretted this answer.

"It *fell* off?" echoed Mrs. Whimpole in disbelief.

"Yes," said Everett, feeling very angry with himself at present. "It does that sometimes. It's my illness, you see — it causes my beard to fall out now and again."

Mrs. Brown and Mrs. Whimpole looked aghast. "But you had such a full beard! You must have been growing it for years!" declared the latter.

"Oh, that?" said Everett. "No, only a few weeks."

Mrs. Brown gasped, and there were so many questions running through her head, but they weren't of the sort a lady usually asks a gentleman. "You poor man," she said. "Are you in very much pain?"

"Oh, yes," said Everett, pitifully. "I grow very weak whenever it falls out, and my face breaks out in a rash."

"Well, it looks all right just now," noted Mrs. Whimpole.

"It takes a few hours," said Everett.

Mrs. Brown and Mrs. Whimpole were so overcome with sympathy for the poor fellow that Charles and Clara could hear them whispering things to one another like "Probably can't afford his medical expenses," "We'll give him a little extra something," and "I'll call Barbara from the DAR. She must know loads of people needing rides. You can't beat these prices," and when the ladies were dropped off at their respective houses, they each gave Everett a hefty tip and a look of utter heartbreak as though they believed him under the most tragic of circumstances.

"Would you look at that!" cried Everett, as Charles and Clara hopped back into the front seat of the car once the last of the ladies was back inside her home. He shook the nearly full change purse he'd used to collect fares.

"*Humph!*" huffed Clara, haughtily. "Don't you pay any attention to him, Charles, dear. He's done a very bad thing," she instructed, still clasping the boy by the hand.

"Oh, come off it!" said Everett.

"And you can stop talking to me like a granny!" added Charles, squinching up his face at her.

"Fine!" said Clara to both of them. "But don't expect me to be happy about the money! You can't keep it, you know — that's pity money!"

"Oh, yes I can!" said Everett, and he puffed out his chest and gave the horn an ornery honk, which startled a nearby pedestrian who jumped out of the car's path as it came barreling back through town.

"The only reason you have all that money is because those ladies from the artillery think you're dying," Clara continued.

"I can't help that!" argued Everett. "They came to that conclusion on their own."

"But you told them you have some horrible beard disease! There's no such thing!"

"We don't know that! For all we know, I might have got it!" said Everett, and Charles who was seated in the middle of the argument looked back to Clara for a rebuttal.

"Ugh!" she cried in distress. "You're only eight-years-old!"

"Look, if you're going to go on acting like a mother hen, next time you can just stay at home!" spat Everett as the car began to climb the hilly field behind their house. But just then the old motorcar began to do some spitting of its own, and there was suddenly quite an awful racket coming from underneath the hood. "Now look what you've done — you've angered the car," said Everett, gripping the steering wheel tight.

"I haven't done anything!" cried Clara, though she was looking rather worried.

"Why's it slowing down?" said Charles as the car's sputtering began to sound much more like hissing and choking.

"How should I know?!" said Everett, and he began bouncing up and down upon the seat as if to say "giddy-up", as there was still quite a bit of hill left for the car to climb.

There was some more choking and hissing, and the car exhaled, sounding as though all the air had been let out of its tires. Then, with one more feeble utterance, it died, and all was silent apart from the worried exclamations of the three children.

"What do we do now?!" moaned Clara. "We can't leave it here — the man with the mustache will know we moved it!"

"No he won't," said Everett, militantly. "We'll push it the rest of the way up the hill. It's our only choice."

Charles and Clara were not without their doubts and grumbles, but they helped all the same, and each of the children stood with their backs to the car and leaned into it with all their might, digging their heels into the grass. When that didn't work, they turned around and pushed.

Everett pushed and said "*Grrrrr!*" Charles pushed and said "*Arghhhh!*" and Clara pushed and said "*Gah!*" and when they'd all managed to be pushing and growling at the same time, the car finally began to move.

"We've got it — keep pushing!" shouted Everett, and they pushed some more.

It would have been quite a funny sight had anyone been watching, for it wasn't everyday you see a tiny man in a bowler hat, a small boy in a cap, and an elderly lady in a hat with decorative fruit pushing an automobile up a hill. In fact, eighty-seven-year-olds are no more likely to be pushing things up hills than they are to be riding in rumble seats. But this was no ordinary day.

"Are we almost there?!" cried Clara, straining to speak and push at the same time.

"Yep!" gasped Everett. "*Just ... one ... more—*"

And with a final *harumph* the car was back where it had always been.

"Oh dear," said Clara. The telephone had gone on ringing all evening and the children sat upon their respective crates in Father's stockroom with no idea whether or not they should answer it.

"We've gotten ourselves into a right mess this time," said Charles. "If that phone keeps ringing, Father'll soon realize, and what if he answers it? He'll know all about the business and how we stole that car."

Everett was perhaps the least concerned. "It can't go on like this forever. They'll soon get tired of us not answering!" he said as the phone jingled another three times upon the wall.

"The man with the mustache will be awfully cross when he realizes his car's broken again — he'll know we did it," said Clara.

"No he won't. He'll just think he hadn't fixed it properly," said Everett. "Though I suspect it's only run out of petrol."

The phone went on ringing. Sometimes it rang two times and sometimes three, and other times it would ring only once, but the children were unable to find any sort of pattern no matter how hard they thought about it.

"Maybe if we picked it up and told them that the company's been bankrupted," said Charles, feeling confident that neither Everett nor Clara would know this word, and that he would have the pleasure of telling them what it meant when they asked, which they did, only he'd rather hoped they'd have sounded a little more impressed — instead they were merely irritated.

"So the next time it rings, we'll pick it up and tell whoever's on the other line that we're no longer in business owing to the driver's illness, which has taken a turn for the worse," said Everett, and the others nodded their heads.

They had only to wait a few minutes before the phone rang once, twice, and once more for a total of three rings.

Everett picked up the receiver and put it to his ear, and he was just about to open his mouth to speak when he heard not one, but *two* voices already conversing on the other end. He listened for only a moment and then placed the receiver back on its hook.

"There's somebody already talking on it," said Everett, curiously.

"Weren't they talking to *you*?" asked Charles.

"I don't think so ... they were going back and forth all by themselves," Everett replied.

"Perhaps it's a party line," said Clara. "My mother and father have one of those."

"What's a party line?" said Everett.

"Well," said Clara, "I think it means that sometimes when you pick up the telephone, there's a party on the other end."

They each thought this through, thinking it might eventually make sense the more they thought of it, but finding that it did not in fact make much sense at all.

"It didn't sound much like a party," said Everett. "Just two people talking."

"There wasn't any music or laughter?" asked Charles.

"Not that I heard," said Everett.

"Try picking it up again and see if they're still there," said Charles.

So Everett picked up the receiver once more and pressed it to his ear.

"Well?" said both Charles and Clara anxiously.

"They're saying something about a woman who wears too much makeup," said Everett, and he continued to listen. "I think the one lady is Missus Brown! She has the same tiny voice," he told them, and hung the phone back up. "It sounds like a private conversation."

"What else were they saying?" asked Charles. "Let's pick it back up."

"But we mustn't," said Clara. "It's impolite to listen in on other people's conversations!'

Everett shot her a dirty look. "You know, you'll break out in a rash of pimples one day being so goodie two-shoes all the time." He then picked up the receiver again and held it up so that both he and Charles could listen in. Clara, meanwhile, sulked atop her crate.

"I've been trying to get ahold of that poor fellow all evening," the boys overheard Mrs. Brown saying. "I'll be needing a ride to the benefit tomorrow, but I haven't been able to reach his agency. I do hope the chap's not fallen ill — he was in quite a state this afternoon. Has some sort of disease that affects his face, poor thing. One minute there was a beard, and the next, there wasn't. I tell you, Evelyn, it was the most pitiful thing!"

"Quick!" whispered Everett to Clara. "They're talking about us."

Clara reluctantly joined them and placed her ear close to Charles and Everett's.

"Odd fellow," continued Mrs. Brown. "Something's stunted his growth — I heard about that sort of thing once on a radio program. Has to do with an iron deficiency or malnutrition or something — darned if I remember."

Charles and Clara began to giggle, but before Everett could say something nasty to them, the stock room door suddenly swung open, and Father came strolling in wearing his night-robe and slippers.

Charles and Everett quickly stepped away from the telephone, which left Clara all alone holding the receiver in a most compromising position.

Father glared sternly down at them with his hands resting on his hips. "Well, that explains it then," he said.

"Pardon me, Father," said Charles, timidly, "but what does it explain?"

"Why there was a charge on the telephone bill, of course — that thing hasn't been used in ages. Now, who have you three been calling?"

Clara looked to Charles and Everett, and both Charles and Everett gulped and looked to one another, each of them seeking answers that no one had yet to think of.

"Clara's been talking to her friend Agnes in Ashford," said Everett, naming the first town to come to mind, which happened to be the next town over from the one they'd lived in in England.

"How does Clara know anyone in Ashford?" asked Father, crossly.

"Um ... pen pals," said Charles.

Father frowned. "Well, I'm sorry, Clara," he said, now a bit more kindly than before, "but if this friend Agnes is a pen pal of yours, I think it best if the two of you continue to exchange messages the old fashioned way — pen and paper," he articulated. And with that he left the room.

"Phew!" said Everett. "I'm glad that's over with. And fancy us not getting a punishment! Good thing it was you making the calls Clara, or else he'd have *really* been mad!"

Clara's face went scarlet, and she stamped her foot. "I was *not* the one making the calls! I don't even know anybody named Agnes!" she wailed.

"Oh, don't be a sourpuss!" said Everett.

"Yes, cheer up!" said Charles. "After all, it's your turn with the turban tomorrow!"

The two boys then turned on their heels and marched up the stairs to bed, and I think, but I'm not quite sure, that Clara had a good cry.

In Which Clara Gives A Piano Recital

The next day, Clara was constantly looking over her shoulder, sure that some horrible tragedy awaited them for having lied. She'd always been told that awful things happened to children who lie, and she wasn't sure if she'd be excused this time or not, seeing as she hadn't actually been the one to tell it. Charles and Everett were much less bothered however, and were annoyed by their cousin's frequent shouts of "What was that?!" and "Do be careful!" or "I suspect the second we step outside it'll begin to rain," which it did, and Clara was then all the more apprehensive.

The bad weather forced them to stay indoors, and seeing as Mother was busy minding baby Isabelle downstairs, the children went upstairs to the nursery for a little privacy. It would have been so much easier if they could have told Mother about the turban, but it's a widely known fact that adults will go to any lengths to deny the existence of magic.

"It's your turn to wear the turban, Clara," Charles and Everett reminded her.

"But I don't want to," she said. "Why can't Charles go first?"

There were two reasons for this. One was that Charles and Everett were being kind in letting Clara go next because that way she could pick a really girly talent that wouldn't frighten her so much. The other reason was that it was raining, and Charles quite selfishly wanted it *not* to be raining while he was having his turn with the turban. The boys, however, told Clara something more like, "Charles might pick something really dangerous and adventuresome, so you had better pick a talent this time if you want to be on the safe side."

"But how are we to make any money when it's pouring down rain?" said Clara.

"We have umbrellas, of course," said Everett.

Clara made up her mind to pick an indoors talent, though she was having quite a lot of difficulty thinking of one. She thought of baking cookies, but no, Auntie Mary would never let her near the oven. Then she thought of being a nurse, but that wouldn't work either as the hospital was much too far away, and she doubted patients would be likely to trust a little girl with such things as taking temperatures and administering medications.

"What's something you've always wanted to do?" asked Charles in an attempt to hurry her along, because waiting around for people to think up talents was a boring business.

"Well," said Clara, "I've always wanted to play the piano. But I don't suppose that makes a lot of money."

"Sure it does!" said Everett. "You could play ragtime in a piano bar like they do in the pictures!"

"I don't think they let children in piano bars though," said Charles.

"Well," said Everett, giving it some more thought, "you could give a recital!"

Charles, too, thought this was a wonderful idea, but Clara was looking less certain.

"I don't know," she said. "Won't everyone be watching me?"

Charles and Everett replied that this was indeed the point of a recital.

"But I'd be awfully nervous!" she said.

"Not with the turban on, you wouldn't," said Everett. "You can do anything you like when you're wearing it."

Clara brightened, for if she wasn't going to feel nervous, she thought she might quite like to give a piano recital. The only question left to answer was *where*? They couldn't very well do it in the house, and they didn't know of any concert halls. Charles suggested that maybe she should play an instrument better suited for travel instead, such as the kazoo or the mouth organ, but Everett didn't think this was such a good idea, and raised a very good point: "Would *you* pay to hear a kazoo or a mouth organ?" And they each agreed that they wouldn't.

"I've had a thought," said Everett. "You know that department store in town? — Woolwarts or something — they have a piano by the escalator. I saw a man playing it once while Mother was shopping for new knitting needles, and people were tossing coins into his hat."

Charles and Clara both liked the sound of this. "And it'd be indoors so nobody would get wet!" said Clara. She especially liked that playing pianos in departments stores didn't sound the least bit dangerous, or even slightly mischievous. In fact, it didn't seem to be any word ending with *ous* at all.

"That's settled then," said Everett. "We'll have to take the streetcar into town."

"Oh, I hope we get to see Frank the conductor again — he was ever so jolly to us!" said Clara, quickly forgetting all about her bad mood.

So the children slipped on their rain coats and galoshes. Charles was then sent to fetch some of Mother's sheet music from the piano bench, and Clara was told to use the bathroom one last time because they all knew what dirty places department store restrooms could be, and while the girl was out of earshot, Everett informed Mother that they were all three going to play over at Bobby Smalls's house and that they'd be back for dinner. It was a good thing Clara didn't hear this, because she'd only just gotten over the last lie they'd told, and this new one was really bad. What if something awful happened and Mother needed to find them? Mothers worry about these things, you know, and it's only good manners to oblige them. Everett knew this, of course, but his heart was so set on helping his parents, and he was even more determined than usual seeing as he hadn't known about telephone calls costing money.

Under the protection of three different-colored umbrellas, the children splashed their way to the streetcar stop, making a game out of jumping over all the biggest puddles. The streetcar was particularly full on this day owing to the rain, but the children were pleased to find Frank again at the controls. He smiled, recognizing them straightaway, and tapped his cheek to welcome a kiss from Clara, who did not hesitate in repeating the act of fondness she'd bestowed upon him their last meeting.

Water dripped onto the aisles and seats of the streetcar as passenger after passenger got on and off, the bad weather trailing in and out behind them, and then Frank called out "Woolworths! Bank! Historical Society!" and the children waved goodbye to him and departed.

They peered out from underneath their umbrellas in search of the department store as business men and women traveled along the busy sidewalks attempting to avoid bumping into one another. Everett was the first to spot the large display windows and green awning of the store, and they quickly entered, shaking off the worst of the rain from their coats and depositing their umbrellas in a bin by the door.

"It's so big!" said Clara, overwhelmed by the many display cases, mannequins and red-colored signs advertising sales and discounts.

There was ladies apparel and hosiery to the left and mens apparel and socks to the right, and at the back of the store were shoes and accessories. The upstairs housed everything else from toys, to housewares, to camping equipment and sporting goods, and at the base of the escalator sat a shiny black grand piano with a velvet cushioned seat.

Directly in front of the children was a man in a white collared shirt and vest, standing behind an ornate gold-plated cash-register.

He smiled down at them. "Looking for something in particular?" he asked pleasantly. The children saw that pinned to his vest was a badge that read "Phil".

All three went to open their mouths in reply when they quickly realized that they had no idea what to say. Clara motioned for Charles to do the talking, and Charles then thought he'd quite prefer Everett to do it instead, and finally after what must have seemed a very awkward amount of time, the eldest of them said, "Might we play your piano?" which wasn't at all what he'd wished to say, but was what nevertheless came out.

Phil's eyes twinkled in amusement. "Well, I'm afraid we can't let just *anybody* play our piano — it was very expensive, you see," he said. "I assume you've had lessons?"

"Not one," said Everett, truthfully, "but Clara here's a child prodigy! Isn't she, Charles?"

Charles, who had not expected to be called upon, diverted his attention from the hypnotic revolving of the escalator, and answered, "Yes!"

"*She's* had lessons, then?" said Phil.

"Well, no. Not exactly," said Everett. "She's picked it up all on her own, haven't you, Clara?"

The girl nodded, though she was feeling very nervous seeing as the turban was still under her coat and not atop her head.

"Well, I don't know," began the man, "I wasn't under the impression it was something you could just 'pick up'," he said.

"She's given recitals all over the place," said Everett.

"All over the world!" added Charles.

"Like where?" asked the gentleman, sounding a little more intrigued.

Everett frowned at Charles, not having intended Clara's notoriety to have extended quite so far. "Well, she debuted with the Coopstown Symphony Orchestra, and just last week she played in Beijing!"

Everyone, including Clara, looked impressed. "My, my," said Phil. "Well, I suppose it wouldn't hurt to hear just one piece, and then if the customers like it, we'll talk."

They followed the man over to the piano and waited for him to open the lid. Clara's stomach was doing somersaults, and when Everett noticed her looking pale and sickly, he said "Put the turban on!" and she complied.

Suddenly, Clara felt a warm tingly feeling running down her back and extending to her fingers. The churning of her stomach quickly subsided, and she soon felt as though she must be of terrible importance in the world, as though she'd become the first lady president, or circumnavigated the globe single handedly in her own aircraft. Not only did she believe herself capable of playing simple songs like "Mary Had a Little Lamb" or "Hot Cross Buns", but she was positively certain that if asked she could transcribe and play Tchaikovsky's entire *1812 Overture* on a single piano, when an hour prior she'd never so much as heard of the composer's name much less his overture.

"Well, my dear girl," said Phil, eyeing the turban as though it made for particularly delightful concert attire. "Have a seat and play us a little something, won't you?"

Clara bowed graciously in acceptance and sat down upon the velvet cushion, smoothing out the pleats of her dress and poising her hands elegantly atop the keys.

Charles held out the several pieces of sheet music they'd brought along, and Clara contemplated them as if old friends. Having made her selection, she regarded the particular piece of sheet music lovingly, as though each of its crinkled pages had brought her hours of enjoyment in the past. It was Chopin's *Minute Waltz*, and without a moment's hesitation, Clara's fingers flew across the keyboard in execution of the opening bars, moving in such a blur that one could hardly tell if the keys had ever been depressed at all.

The melodies swirled out of the piano in perfectly rendered phrases, filling every corner of the store with voluptuous sound. Soon, there wasn't a customer to be found amongst the clothing racks or clearance bins, for they had all gathered as closely as possible around the piano. Then, in just over a minute, the piece came to a close with the striking of a brilliantly bright chord.

The crowd emitted a sigh of euphoria and burst into passionate applause, and Clara, displaying an ease redolent of many years experience, got up from the piano and bowed.

"My dear girl, that was magnificent!" exclaimed Phil, clapping louder than all the rest. "I doubt that piano has ever been played so well in all its years. Will you pleasure us with another selection?"

Clara nodded happily and chose another piece of sheet music, this time Beethoven's *Moonlight Sonata*. Charles and Everett were buzzing with excitement as they watched the crowd of customers grow thicker and thicker, and with a nod of approval from Phil, Charles laid his hat beside the piano for collecting money.

Clara's fingers caressed the keys, the haunting melody rising from the instrument like that of a sorrowful aria rising through a concert hall, never losing the fullness of its tone or the weight of its emotion. The crowd was enraptured as each movement of the sonata was perfectly executed, and when it raced to a finish with a thunderous roar, there was another shower of applause, this time with many shouts of "Brava!" and "Encore!"

Clara bowed again, placing a hand over her chest in a heartfelt gesture, and the sound of clinking could be heard over the din of the crowd as Charles's hat was instantly filled to the brim with coins. Unfazed by all the attention, Clara appeared to posses the confidence of someone twenty years her age, and the crowd of customers, every member of which now having completely abandoned their shopping, continued to grow as more people entered the store and nobody left. They were quiet once again the second Clara seated herself back upon the bench.

"Has anyone a request?" she said, dazzling her fans with a smile.

As though it had been perched on his tongue waiting for the right moment, a man with jet black hair wearing a gray business suit called out "Stars and Stripes Forever!"

Though the piece had not been written for piano, this was no matter, and without any music in front of her, Clara dove right into the keys, pounding out the familiar tune as though she'd composed it herself. Charles and Everett could not believe the tiny girl they'd once considered their dim-witted cousin was now jumping up and down upon the piano, hammering out chords and octaves in a manner wholly resplendent of celebratory bombs and cannons bursting through the air. One could almost picture the flashes of light, and the resulting dark clouds of smoke billowing up in the night sky. Then, with a much brighter and more cheerful rendering, Clara played the jubilant notes typically heard by the piccolos, her fingers sparkling upon the highest keys of the piano, inciting gleeful exclamations and gay laughter from the audience, many of whom were bouncing about on their toes along to the beat of the music.

The final bit of Clara's transcription sounded like the battering of fireworks ricocheting off a body of water, and just when it seemed as though the piano might crack in two, she brought the piece to a glorious finish, looking none the worse for wear as she leapt to her feet and swung herself forward in bow after bow.

The entire store was packed, every inch of it crammed with customers and people simply looking to escape the rain. They'd now filled Everett's hat with coins as well, and the children had begun to collect the excess money in the pockets of their raincoats. As a fitting close to her recital, Clara chose the song "After The Ball Is Over" from Mother's pile of sheet music. The music swirled around the room like the spinning of a carousel, and people swayed buoyantly on their feet, singing along with such gusto that it was a wonder not any one of them had had a drop of alcohol.

With arms slung around one another and shopping bags swinging merrily through the air, the audience members belted out the final words of the refrain "*Aaaaafterrr the baaaaaaaalllllll!*" and collapsed into fits of wild applause and joyous laughter.

A man in a tweed cap stuck two fingers past his lips and gave a shrill whistle, and upon gaining Clara's attention he flung a bouquet of roses at her, having just purchased them from the floral department for this express purpose. Clara caught them with the ease of a wide-receiver and nestled them in the crook of her arm as she continued to wave and bow in receipt of the abundant adulation.

Men and women crowded around her as closely as possible, sometimes reaching out to shake her hand, and other times leaning in to express their personal felicitations. There were offers of patronage from wealthy gentleman, and a group of ladies made mention of starting a scholarship fund in Clara's name. Phil then squeezed his way through the mass of people to greet her. "My heavens, dear girl — I've never seen so many customers in this store in the whole of my life!" he said, gazing about in awe as people spread out around the various departments, having seemingly thought of something they needed whilst in the store. "Could I interest you in giving a weekly concert series here at Woolworths? Fridays, perhaps?"

Everett, who'd been near enough to hear this question, replied, "Fridays is when she takes her tap dance lessons, I'm afraid."

Phil looked astonished. "All that and tapping too! My goodness, well, do come back and play for us sometime, won't you?"

Clara agreed, for it was merely the polite thing to do in these situations and not so much a lie. Charles and Everett then grabbed for her hand, and before the attention of the raucous crowd could get any further out of control, the children ducked low and weaved their way to the front of the store, grabbing for their umbrellas and slipping out the door almost entirely unnoticed.

As they boarded the streetcar a moment later, giving Frank a warm greeting in the process, Charles and Everett held out their hats and pocketfuls of coins to jingle in front of Clara. "What a success!" cried Everett. Though he found it difficult to admit, Clara's piano recital had made them the most money yet, and feeling unusually humbled, he told her as much.

Both boys gave their cousin a hearty slap on the back, and Charles said, "Really nice going! You were *wonderful*!"

"I was?" said Clara, happily. "How marvelous! I wish I could have heard myself play — I just adore piano music!"

The three children were seated in a row, animatedly recounting the best bits of their day as the bumpy streetcar took them home. And, with the turban tucked safely back under her coat, Clara was back to being Clara again.

In Which Charles Becomes A Writer

The rain continued all through the night, and the children went to bed hoping they'd wake up to find it sunny again, but it wasn't. Instead, it rained all through breakfast and the rest of the morning as well, and the children hoped it might stop by lunchtime so that they could go out to play, but it didn't. Then they thought perhaps it might have petered out during the afternoon leaving them a few hours of sunlight before it got dark, but it hadn't.

And so, after supper, there was little choice but to spend the evening in the nursery. Everett suggested they build a fort, and they quickly began arranging furniture and draping old bed sheets over this and that. Boxes, tubs, building blocks, and books were used for such things as the entryway, towers and turrets, and Clara began drawing flowers on pieces of paper to lay out for a garden. Charles had been busy building a staircase out of several volumes of Hans Christian Anderson when he suddenly stopped and sat upon the floor, his fist curled under his chin.

"What's the matter with him?" whispered Clara to Everett.

Everett shrugged. "Hey mate, what's got you rattled?"

Charles didn't answer immediately, and was staring blankly at the floor in front of him. "I think I know what talent I want the turban to give me," he said finally, "only it needs a good think."

"You'll tell us when you've finished having this think, won't you?" said Everett.

"Hmm," said Charles in thought, "maybe. I think I'd better see if I'm any good at it first."

"Good at what?" said Clara.

But Charles didn't answer, and instead got up from the floor and walked right out of the room.

Clara and Everett didn't know what to make of this, and so they continued with the fort's construction, hoping Charles would be in a more forthcoming mood when he returned. A few minutes later, however, they were surprised to find him lugging the black box containing Father's typewriter into the nursery, shutting the door firmly behind him. The turban was already perched atop his head.

"Did you just snatch that from underneath Mother and Father's bed?" asked Everett, pointing to the box.

"Of course not," said Charles, sitting it down upon the floor with a heavy thud. "I simply asked Mother if I could borrow it, and she said yes."

"And she didn't ask what you were doing?" said Everett, quizzically.

"No," said Charles, and it was quite clear from his tone that *they* weren't to ask what he was doing either.

So, slipping a piece of paper into the typewriter, Charles began to type. He started with only a few letters, and when he'd finished with those letters, he had a think, and when that was properly finished, he typed another few letters, and this cycle repeated itself for quite some time.

Clara and Everett were just putting the finishing touches on their fort when it began to seem like there was much less space between the clicks of Charles's letters, and it now sounded as though he were pounding out a steady stream of words, occasionally halting mid-sentence to scratch his head or gaze thoughtfully at the ceiling.

"And you still won't tell us what you're doing?" Everett asked eventually, a twinge of bitterness in his voice.

It took a moment for Charles to register the question, but he only said "*Mmmm,*" which seemed to Everett a clear affirmation.

He and Clara tried to spy on Charles from inside the fort, but Charles quickly turned the typewriter around so they couldn't see the paper.

"He's obviously writing something," said Everett. "He always has fancied himself a writer."

"Perhaps he's writing the great American novel!" said Clara.

Everett wrinkled his nose. "I think that's already been written."

Charles was now typing so steadily that by the time Mother entered the nursery to hurry them off to bed, he'd filled several sheets of paper, all of which he'd placed carefully face-down upon the floor. Mother watched as he yanked another ink-filled page from the typewriter, but to Everett and Clara's disappointment, she didn't demand an explanation of any sort, and merely looked blithely amused.

The next day brought further frustration for Everett and Clara. It continued to rain, and Charles continued to type. They played in the fort until they grew quite sick of it. First, they pretended a tornado had struck and tore bits of it down, and then upon rebuilding it, they jumped up and down upon the floor to simulate an earthquake, and rebuilt it again. Occasionally they'd ask Charles questions or taunt him with jokes and ridicule, but this soon lost its appeal as Charles never showed any notice of it.

Click click click. How tired of clicks they'd become. *Click click click.* Their minds were going mad with the constant sound of clicking, and even when there was a break in the clicking, they thought they could still hear it, like Captain Hook and the ticking of the clock in the belly of the crocodile.

"Do you suppose you'll be quite finished soon?" growled Everett in a moment of particular agitation, but the only response he got was *click click click.*

It pained Everett and Clara to admit that with every click, they found themselves more and more curious what Charles was typing, and more and more angry that he wasn't telling them.

They'd unleashed their anger on the fort, having reduced it to no more than a pile of rubble, when they suddenly heard a very final sounding click. A beautiful silence filled the room, and they looked over to find Charles beaming at a page of paper he'd just pulled from the typewriter.

"Well?" said Everett, hotly.

"I've finished the first chapter!" Charles exclaimed, placing the new page neatly atop the previous ones.

"What?!" cried Everett in indignation. "You mean there's *more*?!"

"Of course!" said Charles. "You never have only one chapter. I figure I'll release them one at a time like Dickens did."

"But you'll need days to do that! Maybe even weeks!" said Clara. "That's much longer than Everett and me had!"

"That should be 'Everett and *I*'," Charles corrected. "And the writing days don't count, only the ones when we're making money."

"How do you figure?" said Everett.

"Well, *you* could drive the second you put the turban on, and Clara could play the piano the second *she* put the turban on. *I* can write the second I put the turban on, but I can't sell anything until I've something written," Charles explained. "Plus, think how much money we'll make selling all seven chapters individually."

162

"*Seven*?!" cried both Clara and Everett.

"A nice number, I thought. Very biblical. Anyhow, I've got the whole book planned out in my head and it *needs* seven chapters."

Everett scowled. "Let us have a look then," he barked.

Charles hesitated, but then handed the tidy pages of his chapter to his brother, who made sure to un-tidy them as soon as he began to read.

Charles and Clara waited anxiously for Everett's verdict. He'd been frowning as he read the first page, clearly trying his best to dislike it, but soon he could no longer contain his interest, and he smiled and laughed, and quickly flipped pages in a hurry to see what would happen next.

"It's *really* good, mate!" said Everett, once he'd finished. "I especially liked the bit where the monkey steals the evil lady's parasol."

"Oh, let me read it!" said Clara, grabbing for the pages. "I love monkeys!"

"We haven't time," said Charles. "Look — the sun's just come out!"

The children claimed a spot on the sidewalk downtown next to a newspaper stand where people were already buying various reading material. They'd decided they couldn't very well type up enough copies of Charles's chapter to sell, so they chose instead for Charles to give a reading, during which they hoped people might toss a few coins in his hat as had been done with Clara and Doggy Swami to great success.

They found an old wooden crate lying in the gutter, and it was quickly snatched for the purposes of a podium.

"Now stand up there," Everett instructed, pointing to the overturned crate. "All you have to do is read, I'll take care of the rest."

Charles straightened the turban atop his head and waited for Everett to give what was sure to be a glittering announcement.

"Ladies and Gentleman!" Everett began. "You are privileged today to witness a reading given by the youngest and most talented writer of the age! Step up! That's right, step up!"

Several street goers stopped and ebbed closer to the children, many of them giggling or commenting on how dear Charles looked in his turban.

"Step *righhht* up! The great author, Charles Sw—" Everett stopped himself, realizing that to give his brother's actual name might be a most unwise thing to do, especially after the trouble with the telephone, which had yet to completely stop ringing. "The great author," he repeated, "Charles, um ... *Lee* Dickens, will now read to you the first chapter from his latest book, *The Woes of Charlotte Pendergrass*."

There was now a handful of people staring up at Charles from the street — a lady with a basket of roses around her arm and a child at each hand, a man in a suit with a pencil behind his ear, an elderly gentleman with a newspaper folded open to the sports section, and a homeless man and his dog.

Charles cleared his throat and held the pages of his chapter out in front of him. "*The Woes of Charlotte Pendergrass*," he read in a clear and steady voice, "by, *me*."

The amusement of the crowd was quickly stifled as the words Charles had written spilled past his lips, floating through the air like a magical spell.

"It was the nicest of times, it was the meanest of times," he began.

There was nothing particularly spectacular about his young voice, but the words he uttered were like nothing the crowd had ever heard before, at least not by a child. There were big words like "impecunious" and "trepidation", and delicate words like "fleeting" and "wistful". His writing reflected the beauty of Shakespeare, yet with an ease of comprehension able to touch the hearts of even the most illiterate of listeners.

The crowd was completely silent, bewitched by the plight of Charles's main character. It was as though every person felt an immediate kinship with Charlotte, experiencing each of her emotions as if their own. Gasps of delight and bouts of laughter accompanied the lighthearted pages of the story, while the most woeful of Charlotte's woes elicited heartbreak and distress. All this was reflected in the faces of the crowd as they clutched at their chests, refusing to exhale until the fate of their heroine was once again secure.

It was with Charlotte's fate that Charles held his power over the ever growing crowd in the days to come. He typed all evening and all morning long, and then read his latest chapter atop the crate downtown at noon each day. By mid-week, the crowd had begun to call him "The Other Dickens", and they arrived early to each reading, some now with blankets and packed lunches as though attending a concert in the park.

Never before were the social classes so united then when listening to Charles read along the very streets their shiny loafers tread to work or their grubby boots scuffled in search of food. They each had in him a friend, someone who understood them and helped them to better understand themselves through the depths of his storytelling. Some deposited coins in the hat laid at Charles's feet if they were able, but the appreciation was never greater than from those who had nothing to give.

"Mr. Dickens, sir," said a man wearing several layers of tattered clothes despite the heat, "I don't no nofink about bein' in love, but Charlotte's devotion to 'er sick 'usband fills a feller's lonely heart. Thank yeh fer reading to us." He bowed and looked regretfully at Charles's hat full of coins, not as though he was suppressing the urge to steal it, but as though he'd have liked very much to have something to place in it.

Then, just as Charles, Everett and Clara were about to leave for the day, the lady with the basket of roses and two children laid a hand on Charles's shoulder. "Thank you, Mr. Dickens," she said, almost in a whisper. "I knows what Charlotte's feeling right now ... I was like her once, you know — went through somethin' similar when my husband was dying right after these two little ones here was born." She wrapped her arms around her son and daughter's shoulders and squeezed. Then, blinking back a stray tear, she smiled at Charles. "You write Charlotte a happy ending for us now, won't you?"

Charles felt a weight in his chest and could only nod in reply, for this was more than anyone had ever asked of him, but that evening when he sat down to type, the words cascaded from his fingers faster and more poignant than ever before.

With the end of the week came the conclusion of Charles's novel, and gazing down from atop his crate, it looked as though the entire town was standing in the street before him. They'd all shown up for a happy ending, and for the first time all week, Charles felt a pang of nervousness despite the turban as they cheered him on, clapping and banging upon trash can lids, and whistling through their teeth. As soon as Charles held the pages of his chapter out in front of him, the crowd fell silent, and not even the jingle of a shop door opening and closing could be heard as he began to read.

Charles's words strung together in sentences that ebbed and flowed like a river, or like beautifully shaped phrases of a song. The faces within the crowd were frozen in anticipation, as though they were listening to a doctor's diagnosis of a sick loved one, and then, weaving the threads of Charlotte's story into a magnificent tapestry, Charles's novel came to a close and he stepped down from the podium. Charlotte, a lonely and bitter woman whose bank had gone under along with all her life savings, had overcome poverty and the death of her husband when a town came together to show her the true meaning of human kindness.

The crowd exhaled in delight. Many were wiping their eyes with handkerchiefs, and the lady with the roses was hugging her children close. Filled with joy, they clapped and cheered, throwing coins and flowers at Charles as he took a dignified bow, and there were shouts of "A masterpiece!" and "The greatest writer of the age!" or "Long Live Charles Lee Dickens!"

Hoards of people clamored for Charles's attention, shaking hands with him, patting him on the back, and asking all sorts of questions about publication and future books, the answers for which Charles politely evaded knowing he wouldn't write again until he could do so without the aide of the turban. The lady with the roses kissed him on the cheek, and then behind her an elderly gentleman who had attended every single reading pressed through the crowd. He was wearing an expensive looking suit with a shiny timepiece dangling from his vest pocket. He beamed down at Charles, his eyes twinkling through a pair of pince-nez glasses.

"That was truly remarkable, young man!" the man bellowed in a low, rumbly sort of voice. "Almost *un*believably remarkable," he added with a wink.

Charles suddenly felt slightly uncomfortable, wondering if the man somehow knew about the turban, but of course he could not.

"I see you've made quite a lot of money there," he said, eyeing the hat full of coins at Charles's feet which had been filled each day upon the conclusion of his reading by appreciative business people and shoppers.

"Yes ... but I can't keep it," said Charles, and he turned to Everett and Clara beside him as if to seek their permission, but they offered no objections. "We were trying to make money for our parents, you see — my father's grocery store was burned down by the Ku Klux people, and he can't find enough work ... but after meeting all these folks here this week, some of them that don't even have enough food or a place to sleep, I realize they need it so much *more* than we do ..."

For a moment the man said nothing, regarding Charles with a faint smile. "Keep your money," he said finally. "Your story has inspired hope and justice in our hearts, and I now feel a generosity I've never felt in all my years. I will be donating a substantial sum in your name to the homeless shelter, and seeing as I am one of the town governors, I think I might have it in my power to convince a few people here today to join me in creating a task force to improve working conditions and job availability for the underprivileged in our town." He leaned in closer to Charles. "And I usually achieve what I set out to do," he said with another wink. "Thank you, Mr. Dickens, for your story!" And with this sentiment, the gentleman tipped his hat to Charles and hobbled back into the crowd.

Charles beamed. It was the best he'd ever felt. It was the best Everett and Clara, and many others in the town had felt in a very long time as well, especially the homeless man who was now sharing a sandwich with his dog, for truly there is very little so fulfilling as sharing happiness with others.

Removing the turban from his head, Charles followed Everett and Clara home, clutching the pages of his book to his chest.

"Don't put the typewriter away yet!" said Everett as Charles was about to lower the machine into its box.

"Why?" asked Charles. "I'm not going to write another book for a long while."

"No, no — it's not that," said Everett. "I've had a thought. Now that we've each made some money, we should probably be giving it to Mother and Father so they can be using it."

"But what's that got to do with the typewriter?" asked Charles.

"Well, I was thinking we could pretend that Father's uncle, the Baron, left Father some money. You could type up a letter explaining as much, and then we'll send it to Father in the post. It's the only way they'll take the money — if they knew *we'd* made it, they'd make us give it back!"

"But won't Mother and Father wonder why the money wasn't just sent along with the trunk?" said Charles.

"*No*," Everett assured him. "The Baron was *crazy*! They won't think anything of it."

So Charles set to work on typing up a letter while Everett and Clara were busy counting all the money they'd each made. On more than one occasion, Charles had to start over again on a new sheet of paper, and likewise, Everett and Clara lost count a couple of times and were forced to start back at the beginning. Not surprisingly, they were all thoroughly bad tempered by the time they'd managed to finish their respective tasks.

"Well?" said Charles. "How much money did we make?"

"Seven-hundred-and-eighty-two dollars!" exclaimed Everett.

"And twenty-three cents!" added Clara.

"Yippee!" cried Charles. "I bet we could live off that for ages!"

"Let's read your letter," said Everett, and he and Clara peered down at the page of paper sticking out of the typewriter.

```
Dear Nephew Edward and family,

I'm sorry that I'm dead. I miss
you. I hope you miss me too.
Here is some money I would like
you to have. It's a lot. It
should last you a really long
time if you're careful. Don't
spend it all at once. Heaven's
nice. Hope everything's good
down there.

Lots of love,
His Lordship, Uncle Baron
```

"Hmm," said Everett. "It's not quite as good as your book."

"That's cause he's not wearing the turban!" said Clara, pointing to Charles's bare head.

Charles ran his fingers through his hair and sighed. "Shoot, I hadn't thought of that."

"Never mind," said Everett. "I doubt the Baron was very good at letter writing. Should it say 'Uncle Baron' though? Didn't he have a name?"

"I suspect so," said Charles, "but I don't know it if he did."

"Oh well," said Everett. "We'll take it to the post office with the money in the morning."

And this is exactly what the children did, though the post office felt an awful long way away considering they were lugging seven-hundred-and-eighty-two dollars and twenty-three cents in coins in two buckets they'd taken from the nursery, which on any other day contained Lincoln Logs.

The buckets were too heavy for one person to carry by themselves for very long, so Clara went back and forth from helping Everett with his bucket to helping Charles with the other, an exercise which drew quite a bit of attention from passers by.

"Almost there!" said Everett, his face turning purple from the strain of his bucket.

The post office door loomed ahead, and a lady with a very curious smile on her face was kind enough to hold the door open for them on her way out. At the counter was an older woman with her hair up in a bun and a monocle on a chain around her neck.

As the children approached, she held the monocle up to her eye and peered at them through it as if viewing some sort of rare specimen. "Good heavens!" she cried at the sight of the buckets' contents. "You children must be looking for the bank! It's three doors down on the right." But when moments later the children were still at the counter, she said, "Surely you don't mean to mail that money ..."

"But we do, actually," said Charles, placing his bucket on the floor and rubbing his back with his stiff hands.

"Don't worry," said Everett at the woman's look of surprise. "We're only looking to send it a few blocks away."

"Why don't you deliver it yourselves then? It'd cost much less money," said the woman.

"Because it's a surprise," answered Clara.

The woman squinted at them. "You know, paper bills would be much lighter," she said.

"That's alright," said Everett. "We'd like to send the coins anyway. We have plenty of money for the postage."

The woman scowled but called for a gentleman in the back to come around front and help her package the coins in a crate, which the man later hammered down after the children had placed Charles's letter atop the money and removed the ten-dollars they needed for postage.

They then left the post office, completely oblivious to the looks of incredulity they were being given by the staff and patrons, and they rushed home, hopeful that the money would arrive very soon.

"Mother and Father will be so pleased," said Charles, happily. And they each agreed that they couldn't wait to see their faces when the crate was opened.

In Which Watson Makes His Parents Proud

Mother and Father's faces had looked exactly as the children had hoped they might when they opened the crate and saw all the money. The fact that the letter had apparently been composed in heaven, or that the money was all in coins was thankfully of no concern to Father. "How like Uncle to send a trunk full of coins from beyond the grave!" he'd said. Father vowed to abide by his uncle's wishes and not spend the money too quickly, and Charles found this all rather funny because he'd of course only made that part up.

For a whole ten minutes everyone was very jolly — Mother and Father were relieved that they now had some extra money to support the family while Father continued to look for work, and the children were overcome with giddiness at having done something so clever and wonderful. They felt the secret bubbling up inside them like a fizzy drink — it was the same sort of feeling you get when you know somebody's getting a surprise party and you want to tell them because you think how fun it would be to surprise them, but you can't because then the party wouldn't truly be a surprise after all! The only difference between surprise parties and the children's secret was that they'd *never* be able to tell anybody *ever*, but they tried not to let this upset them because Charles had read somewhere in the Bible or on a box of Cracker Jacks once that the humblest sort of people do good deeds without any expectation of praise or reward.

Now you're probably wondering why I said everyone was jolly for only ten minutes, and to specify, Mother and Father went on feeling jolly all day — it was the children who were soon in distress.

It started out the simplest of matters. Watson (who should not be forgotten for he was very much there and just as jolly as everyone else) said he was going to the bank, and Father quite nicely asked him if he wouldn't mind depositing the trunk full of coins seeing as he was going anyway, and Watson was very happy to oblige. Only, just as Watson was about to leave, Mother reminded him that it was an unusually chilly day and that he'd best wrap up. Clara, who'd unraveled the turban a few hours earlier, pretending she was an Indian princess with a silk veil, had hung the length of periwinkle fabric over the back of a chair, and Mother, thinking it was a scarf, had picked it up and slung it around Watson's neck.

The children had nearly jumped out of their skin at the sight of such a thing, but they could hardly say "Wait! Don't take our magic turban!" To make matters worse, Watson was mumbling something about how every time he went to the bank he was reminded of his parents, and then just as he was stepping out the door, he turned to Mother and said, "I wish I'd become a banker like Mamma and Papa wanted." Then the door closed behind him, and the children were left scrambling for their shoes and jackets, making silly excuses of being late for a play date with Jimmy Holbrook before dashing out the door after Watson, who they thought by this point was surely thinking he was very much a banker on his way to the bank.

"Oh, this is dreadful! What a thing to happen!" cried Clara.

"It was *you* that left the thing on the back of that chair," grumbled Everett as they hurried down the street, trying to keep an eye on Watson without his knowing.

They followed him all the way into town and through the bronze plated doors of the Coopstown Savings and Loan. Watson had walked into the building looking as proud as though his name were emblazoned on the side of it, and just inside the door he waved to a woman seated at a desk behind a glass partition and said, "Good morning, Martha!" The woman waved politely back, but the look on her face confirmed that she hadn't a clue who Watson was.

The children ducked behind a potted plant. "How does he know who she is?" whispered Charles.

"I've no idea," said Everett. "Maybe they went to school together."

"No, silly, black people go to different schools," said Charles.

"Really?" said Clara. "That's stupid."

"I know!" agreed Charles. "Father says it's just plain prejulistism," he said, knowledgeably.

"Quit yapping, you two — we've got a real problem here!" hissed Everett.

Watson had walked toward the front of the large marble hall where several men in suits were standing behind sets of gold bars with little slots for people to deposit or collect their money. Some of the men were scribbling things in ledgers, and others were counting bills or stamping things on pieces of paper. The children were silently praying that Watson would simply deposit Father's money and leave, but they quickly realized that this was hardly his intention.

"Good morning, gentlemen!" said Watson briskly to the first teller he saw. "You've been expecting me, I'm sure."

The puny man stuttered momentarily, looking as though he were trying to remember if he'd been quite expecting anyone at all. "I'm sorry?" he said.

"Yes, I can see I've taken you by surprise. Well, the Chairman will be hearing about this ... someone clearly hasn't been doing their job. Makes no matter, however — as long as everything is running ship-shape with your branch, we've nothing to worry about."

The gentleman on the other side of the gold bars was now looking terribly worried.

"Allow me to introduce myself. Watson Harris, Chief Undersecretary to the United States Federal Reserve System's Chairman of the Board," he said importantly, slipping his hand through the bars to shake the teller's hand. "Pleased to meet you, I'm sure. Martha's looking well! Dear woman — met her at a conference a few years back."

The children gaped at one another in horror, and Clara was biting her bottom lip so hard it had turned purple. "What are we going to do?!" she cried.

"*Chief Undersecretary*? Where'd he come up with that?!" said Everett. "We've got to get that turban away from him!"

"No we *can't*!" said Charles, brushing a palm leaf out of his face. "He clearly thinks he's somebody important. He'd probably fight us! Remember all the fuss baby Isabelle put up when we tried to take the turban away from her? And she was only an infant!"

The teller had nearly jumped out of his skin at Watson's declaration and ran around to a side door to greet him, muttering a lengthy and ill-worded apology while shaking Watson's whole arm with the enthusiasm of a golden retriever. Many of the other tellers had followed closely behind, lining up behind the first like a troop of butlers in service to the Queen's estate.

"Mr. Undersecretary, sir, I beg your forgiveness! The proper personnel was not informed of your visit. I'm sure it's all a misunderstanding — we'll do our utmost to accommodate you! Though we'd have put out the welcome mat, so to speak, had we known to expect the pleasure ahead of time, of course," he quipped, laughing jovially all the while sounding thoroughly disingenuous. "May I take your coat?" he asked. "And there's coffee and light refreshments in the back."

The children held their breath, hoping Watson would hand over his coat and scarf, even if it would mean him getting into trouble when he suddenly had no idea what a chief undersecretary did without the turban wrapped around his neck. This hope was futile, however.

"I'll keep my coat, thank you. There's quite a draft in here, don't you think?" said Watson, officiously.

"You're quite right, sir," replied the teller without hesitation. "We're usually very warm in here — perhaps the heat could be turned on. Rather chilly weather for this time of year. We'll telephone the janitor straightaway."

"Yes, that's probably best," agreed Watson with a perfunctory nod. "Well, you all go about your business. I'll just be floating around today in a purely supervisory capacity so as to report back to the Chairman of the Board on the efficiency of your branch. Oh, and before I forget, please deposit this money into the account of Edward Swope for me," said Watson, not sounding at all like himself. He held out the crate of coins, ignoring the momentary flash of bafflement across the teller's face. "A thousand thanks, my good man."

"Of course, your Undersecretaryship — I mean, *Mr.* Undersecretary!" said the man, followed by a nervous high-pitched laugh. "What an honor to have your business at our humble branch! I'll deposit this for Mr. Swope immediately." He scurried off, holding the crate out in front of him as if it contained the royal family jewels.

Watson then began to pace around in front of the teller stations and behind, observing the bank staff at their work while nodding and scratching his chin. Sometimes he would mutter things like "hmm," and "ah ha", or "huh" and "very curious", or "*interesting*", causing all the tellers within earshot quite a lot of anxiety, and other times he'd jot down notes in a pad of paper he'd taken from inside his jacket, the menacing sound of his pencil point as it scribbled upon the paper causing even more anxiety among the gentleman than did his commentary.

The children crouched lower behind the tall branches of the potted plant so as not to be spotted by the nosing Watson or the occasional customer entering and leaving the bank.

"I suppose it's all rather harmless," whispered Everett. "He'll just have a look round and then leave, and before he can go sending any report to the Chairman of the Board, we'll get the turban back from him."

"I hope you're right," said Charles.

"He *is* very convincing as an undersecretary, whatever that is!" agreed Clara.

Watson was now chatting up Martha, whom he was still claiming to have met before, and of course Martha, now aware of his prestigious title, had no choice but to pretend that she remembered their last meeting with extreme fondness. When he'd entered her office area at the back of the bank, she'd leapt up from her desk and curtsied.

"Mr. Undersecretary! Nigel's just informed me of the purpose for your visit," she said, referencing one of her tellers, for it was indeed *her* bank seeing as she was the branch manager. "Please, have a seat at my desk — consider it yours while you're here," she said, motioning to her leather desk chair and straightening her necktie.

"Why, thank you, Martha," said Watson, and after first appraising the leather chair, he took a seat. Then, fully relinquishing her status, Martha seated herself on a much smaller chair in front of her desk meant for customers.

To the children, Watson and Martha's conversation was merely a conglomeration of imperious looks from Watson and appeasing smiles from Martha (though Charles thought he heard a few impressive words like "dividends" and "semi-annual" thrown about), and once they were convinced that Watson couldn't get himself into too much trouble in her office, they turned their attention toward two tellers near the front who were whispering back and forth to one another in apparent excitement. They were standing only a few paces away from where a telephone hung on the wall.

"I tell you, Nigel, this is the biggest thing to happen to us since that time Woodrow Wilson deposited a check at teller station number three!" said the one gentleman to the other, hardly able to control his volume.

"*Shh!*" hissed Nigel, whom the children recognized as the puny man who'd first greeted Watson. "We don't want to get written up in his report for gabbing during operating hours! But it *is* very exciting of course, especially with that new bank opening up across the street and stealing half our business."

"If only there were a way to let customers know we've had a visit from the Chief Undersecretary to the

United States Federal Reserve System's Chairman of the Board!" said the nameless teller with great clarity, having rehearsed Watson's title over and over again in his head until he could say it with the pontifical air it was due. "Customers wouldn't want to do their banking anywhere else!"

Nigel pursed his lips. "That's providing he gives us a good review."

"But of course he will! We keep this bank running marvelously, and you heard how well he spoke of Martha — he wouldn't report anything that might jeopardize her career!"

"Hmm," said Nigel. "We'll see."

"Listen — I've got a friend down at *The Aegis* who works in the newsroom. One telephone call, and we could have a reporter right here in the bank within a matter of minutes!" said the teller persuasively.

"Absolutely not!" Nigel scoffed. "That's a recipe for disaster if ever I heard one!"

"Don't *worry*," pleaded the other man. "He won't print anything I don't want him to — we're old chums from way back!"

The children could tell Nigel was quickly softening, and they didn't like it one bit. "Well ... it *would* be good publicity. And that new bank would *hate* it," said Nigel, almost giggling at the thought. "Alright! You make the phone call, and I'll go refill Mr. Harris's coffee so he's in a right chipper mood when the reporters get here!"

Charles, Everett and Clara were in a terrible panic as they heard the other teller clearly annunciating the number of the newspaper office into the telephone.

"I just knew that turban was trouble!" cried Clara, biting at her nails.

"Oh, puh-*lease*!" said Charles. "Just this morning you were twirling around with it draped over you like some ding-bat Arabian princess."

"*Shut up*, the pair of you!" spat Everett. "We've got to get Watson out of here before the newspeople arrive!" he said.

"But how?" exclaimed Charles.

Everett grimaced in thought. "What we need is a diversion," he said a moment later.

"What sort of diversion?" said Clara.

"I haven't thought that far ahead yet," said Everett, and when Clara went to speak again, he shushed her and continued to think.

"*I* know!" said Charles, and before he could be shushed himself, he added, "One of us could yell 'Fire!'. Then, once everyone's outside, we can snatch Watson's turban and sneak off with him before the others realize he's gone."

Both Everett and Clara looked as though they wanted to discount this idea — Everett because *he* hadn't thought of it, and Clara because it seemed awfully wrong to yell "Fire" when there wasn't actually a fire anywhere at all. But Everett couldn't think of a better idea, and so he agreed, and of course once Charles and Everett were in agreement about something, it rarely mattered what Clara thought.

"Now," said Everett to Charles, clearly about to give orders, "Clara and I will run out awhile, and you stay back to yell 'Fire!' — but make sure you scram the second you've done it or else Watson might see you!"

"Right," said Charles with an affirmative nod.

"Good luck then, mate," said Everett. "Have done with it, and then meet us back outside. We'll hide by the door to wait for Watson to appear, and when he does, we'll kidnap him and head straight for home."

With that, Everett and Clara checked to make sure nobody was looking and then slipped out from behind the potted plant and out the door without a peep.

Charles suddenly felt alone and very nervous, and he took several deep breaths before resigning himself to his task. Then, stepping out from behind the plant, he mustered up the courage he'd need to yell—

"FIRE!"

Charles pressed his fingers to his lips as if to check that they were still closed, and indeed they were. Someone had snatched the word right out of his mouth! He quickly surveyed the room, at which point he spotted Nigel shrieking and pointing to a spot on the floor against the wall. "Fire! Fire!" the man cried again, waving for the other tellers to abort their stations. "Everybody out!"

To Charles's great surprise, thick gray smoke was rising up in steady vapors from the iron grate in the floor. Therefore, not allowing himself another thought about the uncanny occurrence, Charles pushed through the doors of the bank just as Watson and Martha came storming out of the office.

"*Over here!*" shouted Everett in a whisper, which is quite a hard thing to do if you've never tried it before.

Everett and Clara had their backs flat up against a pillar, and they were peering around the side of it so as to spot Watson the second he appeared. "Did it work?" asked Everett, as Charles slipped in between them.

He had only a few seconds to explain how he'd never gotten around to yelling "Fire!" at all because someone had already yelled it, and then the bronze front doors of the bank burst open to emit Nigel and a handful of other petrified tellers who were scrambling out in hysterics, wheezing and coughing dramatically.

The children could hear Watson's gruff voice yelling something from inside the bank. "*Out*, Martha! Leave it to me! I can't let one of the Chairman's banks go up in flames!"

"Oh, NO!" cried each of the children.

"What an *idiot*!" spat Everett, disgusted by their own bad luck. "Now the fool's gonna go and get himself cremated!"

Clara couldn't help herself, the thought of Watson dying a horrible death by fire sent tears streaming down her face. "Oh, what a thing to happen!" she said again, for she frequently said this when a thing happened that she wished hadn't.

"Wait — *listen*!" said Everett. The sound of a bell clanging could be heard over the din of the crazed tellers, and it seemed to be getting louder and louder.

"That sounds like the fire bell!" said Charles.

"You don't suppose—" began Everett, but before he could finish the question, a bright red fire engine came barreling around the corner with several fireman hanging off the sides of it.

"Hooray! They called the fire department!" cried Clara. "Watson won't die a horrible death after all!"

As the truck came to a screeching halt outside the bank building, several firefighters in helmets jumped from the vehicle and raced up the marble steps to the front doors, yanking a leather hose behind them. The tellers backed away to let the firefighters pass, but before they could enter the building, Watson stepped calmly out the door holding his hands up in front of him so as to block their path.

"Hold it!" he said, speaking the two words in such a firm tone that not one of the firefighters dared take another step forward. "I'm afraid I've rendered your services unnecessary. It seems there was a little problem with the heater — it was a bit chilly, you see, and they turned it on for me — but I've switched it back off and there's been no harm done."

"Mr. Undersecretary, sir! We're most obliged to you! I assure you the heater has been properly maintained — this is a *most* freak occurrence!" said the puny teller, edging his way closer to Watson.

"Never you mind, Nigel," said Watson, dully. "I hardly think the Chairman will be greatly concerned with the small matter of a heater malfunction."

The fireman nearest to Watson grunted. "You won't mind if we give it a check, will yeh? Being's we're here an' all."

"By all means," said Watson, stepping aside.

The children could see no method of kidnapping Watson while he remained surrounded by the assembly of grateful tellers, but they felt sure that something terrible was bound to happen if they didn't somehow manage to get him away from the bank as soon as possible. This fear was well warranted, for just as Martha was offering Watson her profound thanks, a man in a fedora and trench coat raced up the steps followed closely by another man toting a camera with a large flash.

"My word! What's all the commotion?" said the man, holding a notepad and pencil at the ready.

The teller who'd placed the phone call to the newspaper office leapt forward. "We've had a fire! And the Chief Undersecretary to the United States Federal Reserve System's Chairman of the Board *saved* the bank!" the teller exclaimed in what he would forever consider a very proud moment.

"My, my," said the man in the fedora with a smug grin. "Henry — I smell a front page!" he told the cameraman.

Then, all in a matter of seconds, there was a click and a flash of bright white light, and if only Watson's parents had been alive the next morning when the newspaper arrived, they'd have been very, very proud.

In Which Watson Makes The Front Page

There it was. Just as they'd feared. Watson's face was beaming back at the children from the front page of the morning newspaper. In the picture, he was flanked by Martha, Nigel, a stray fireman, and the teller who'd placed the telephone call to the newspaper office. The article's headline read:

**FIRST BLACK CHIEF UNDERSECRETARY
TO THE UNITED STATES FEDERAL
RESERVE SYSTEM'S CHAIRMAN OF
THE BOARD SAVES COOPSTOWN
SAVINGS AND LOAN FROM FIRE!**

The headline was in such big lettering and was so lengthy that besides it and the picture, barely anything else fit on the front page.

"Lucky we got up early," said Everett, who was holding the dewy newspaper out in front of him.

"But how are we ever going to explain this to Father?" said Charles, worriedly.

"We're *not* going to explain it — that's how!" said Everett.

"But he always reads the paper at breakfast! He'll go looking for it if it's not there," Charles argued.

"We'll just tell him that Peter must have missed our house today when he was delivering the papers."

"I think Father'll be suspicious," said Charles. "He may even go next door and ask if they've gotten *their* paper!"

"That's why we're going to go round and snatch them all up before anyone can read them — we don't want the neighbors seeing Watson's face in the paper either! It's still early, and Peter's just made his deliveries, so we should be able to retrieve most of them — come on!"

Clara and Charles followed Everett through the neighborhood to steal the newspapers from each front lawn, and as the sky grew distinctly less gray and considerably more bright, they began to feel very conspicuous.

"I don't like this at all," moaned Clara, clutching several damp newspapers to her chest and staring anxiously up at the surrounding houses. "What if somebody sees us?"

"Would you rather them see Watson in the newspaper?" replied Everett.

Clara didn't respond, for neither option was at all appealing.

"Only a few more left," said Everett as they neared Grouchy Mr. Granger's house at the bottom of the street. They'd saved his house for last because it was the farthest away, and because going anywhere near it always required plucking up some courage.

It figured that Peter had thrown the paper quite a ways up Grouchy Mr. Granger's steep front lawn, and so a trembling Clara was made to collect it, owing to Charles and Everett's arguing that she was the smallest and also the least visible in her dark pea coat.

Just as Clara's fingers quivered over the newspaper, the porch light flickered on and the front door swung open to reveal Grouchy Mr. Granger in his night robe, wearing a fowl expression.

"*RUN!*" shouted Everett, and in a flash he and Charles were off up the street.

Clara felt her heart jolt in her chest, and she grabbed for the newspaper. Then, without a look behind her, she ran as fast as her little legs could manage, nearly toppling down the lawn and into the street with echoes of "What do you children think you're doing?!" ringing in her ears.

There was nothing on the children's mind but to escape, and when they made it back to their house and finally dared to look behind them, they were relieved to see that they hadn't been chased. They were each hunched over, one hand on their knee, and the other clutching the stitches in their sides.

190

"*That ... was ... a ... close ... one!*" gasped Everett.

Charles agreed, for even though Mr. Granger had been nice to him at Halloween, stealing his newspaper felt like something altogether different.

Once they'd caught their breath, there was then the matter of hiding the newspapers someplace where Father was sure not to find them.

"We could burn them," suggested Charles.

Everett shook his head. "There's too many — people would see the smoke."

Clara then suggested they stash the papers in the rumble seat of the old motor car, and this seemed as good a place as any seeing as nobody but the children ever bothered with the car, and the man from Philadelphia wasn't coming down to buy it for another week.

"Now, just act casual," Everett instructed once they had gotten rid of the papers and were entering the house. Poncho greeted them at the door, and he sniffed them so suspiciously it was almost as if he knew what they'd done.

"Morning!" said Father, sounding rather chipper as he bounded down the stairs for his breakfast. He'd been extra cheerful ever since the money from the Baron had arrived. "You're out and about awfully early!" he commented.

"Yes," said Everett quickly.

Father paused a moment on the bottom step as though he were waiting for an explanation, but Everett simply smiled back at him uncomfortably.

"Well then, I'll just dash out to get the paper," he said, nonchalantly.

"*No!*" yelped Clara.

If looks could kill, Clara would have been very much dead. "What Clara *means*," stammered Everett, still glowering at his cousin, "is that we've already checked."

"That's right," said Charles. "We thought we'd bring it in for you! But when we looked it wasn't there."

Father squinted his eyes at them in contemplation. "Well — if you don't mind, I think I'll just make sure," he said, and as soon as he was out the door, Everett and Charles rounded on Clara.

"Could have given us away!" shot Everett, and Charles added that Father had looked very strangely at them, but they quickly stopped hounding her for tears had begun to fill the girl's eyes and they couldn't stand the thought of another one of *those* scenes.

"Oh, fine, you're forgiven," said Everett irritably after Clara wailed an apology. "But not another word about papers!"

To the children, it felt as though the past day had been comprised of one close call after another, which is a terribly exhausting way to feel. Thankfully, once they'd finally snatched the turban from around Watson's neck and yanked him out of sight before the bank staff was any the wiser, he'd forgotten about the whole ordeal. "I must'a ate som'n funny," he'd said, back to speaking with his usual inelegance. "The whole afternoon feels like a blur!" The children had tried to placate him, simply agreeing with everything he said, and he'd continued to mumble to himself the entire walk home. "There's all these crazy thoughts floatin' through my head, but ... nah!

It must'a been dem expired pickles I had earlier!" he'd said, scratching at his head.

Now the children were at the table having their breakfasts when Father entered the kitchen a few minutes later looking thoroughly lost without his newspaper.

"Huh," he said. "You kids were right. Couldn't find it anywhere."

All three children nodded knowingly and diverted their eyes back to their bowls of oatmeal.

"Find what, dear?" asked Mother, who was cleaning up a mess of mashed bananas baby Isabelle had slopped onto the floor.

"The paper," replied Father, still with a blank look upon his face. "Next door's missing theirs too. He was out searching his lawn same as I was."

"Oh well," said Mother casually. "Peter's probably just fallen ill or something. We all have our off days."

Father merely grunted in response and sat down at the table to his plate of eggs and toast, but he did not seem his usual self at all. He ate a few pieces of toast and sighed, and then a few forkfuls of eggs followed by another sigh, and the children were feeling increasing nervous about his behavior.

"You know," he said, after only half finishing his breakfast. "I think I'll just go and buy the paper from the grocery store in town. Mornings don't seem quite the same without a paper, somehow."

"Alright, dear," said Mother, hardly paying any notice.

Everett nearly choked on a mouthful of oatmeal he'd yet to swallow. "*We'll* go for you, Father!" he volunteered in desperation.

Father gave him a pat on the back. "That's very kind, son, but I think I'd better go all the same — I'm nearly out of shoe polish."

"Then we'll come with you!" Everett retorted before Father could make it out the door.

Charles nudged him in the side. "*What for?*" he hissed. "So we're in hitting distance when he spots the newspaper?!"

"Come along, then," said Father, stepping outside and holding the door open behind him.

"Oh, we'll think of something on the way," Everett whispered back to Charles. "We can't let him see that paper!"

"Right," Clara agreed, for she wanted to be included, and she always found agreeing with Everett much easier than making up her own mind about things.

The children followed warily behind Father into town, nervously holding their breath every time he waved hello or tipped his hat to someone passing in the other direction, for nearly everyone appeared to have a newspaper about them. Thankfully, Father was set on having his own paper however, and didn't bother any of the passers by for a look. He did stop for a quick chat with Old Mrs. Mulberry though, who was just on her way back from the store with her daily nectarine, and while she was telling Father how much she missed his little store, the children frantically weighed their options.

"We could tell him Watson's got a look-a-like!" said Clara.

"He'd never believe that," Everett protested. "He'd recognize Watson's coat. Plus, he saw Mother put that turban around Watson's neck!"

Clara frowned.

"What about a diversion?" said Charles.

But what sort of diversion Charles had in mind they did not find out, because Mrs. Mulberry's update on her cat Harriet's health troubles was unusually short, owing to her needing to return home to administer the cat's medication.

"Keep up, children!" said Father, who had gotten several paces ahead of them while they were busily murmuring back and forth to one another and trying to keep their distance.

"Ohhh! *Do* something!" Clara whispered to Everett as Father was just about to open the glass door of Tate's Grocery.

They followed him inside, glancing around the entire store for the newspaper and magazine racks.

"Found them!" said Charles in Everett's ear, and he pointed to the back left-hand corner of the store.

A jolly-faced gentleman with scads of wrinkles and a brilliantly shiny silver head of hair then greeted them with a "Hello!" and a wave from behind the counter where hundreds of canned goods were stacked neatly on shelves along the wall.

Before Father could reply, Everett called out "Hello Mr. Grocery Store Owner!" for what else do you call a man who owns a grocery store when you don't know his name? "My father here used to own a grocery store too, but it burned down!"

Father looked aghast at Everett's outburst and smiled apologetically to the man behind the counter as Charles and Clara slipped quietly to the back of the store to locate the incriminating papers.

"Well, I'll be! That there's the most terrible thing I've a'heard in days!" said the gentleman, who introduced himself as Mr. Tate. "You must've been devastated! *Juuuh-st* devastated!"

Father then muttered a few concessions, and the two men were soon chatting like colleagues, for it wasn't every day that Father had another grocer to talk to, and everybody knows how nice it is to have somebody to whom you can say things like "Do you know so-and-so?" and "Have you heard of this-or-that?" or "I hate it when that happens" and "I know just what you mean!"

With Father sufficiently distracted, Everett ducked down the first of the two little aisles in search of shoe polish, and he soon spotted Charles and Clara stuffing bundles of papers behind a stack of Old Dutch Cleanser tins.

"Oh good, you've found them!" said Everett.

"Got them all, I think!" said Charles, re-stacking the few tins they'd knocked over in the process.

"Well done!" said Everett. He then grabbed the first can of shoe polish he could find and motioned for Charles and Clara to follow him back to the front of the store.

"We've found your shoe polish for you, Father!" said Everett when there was a break in the two gentlemen's conversation.

Father glanced down at the contents of Everett's outstretched hands. "That's very thoughtful of you children. And it's my brand and everything," he said with a smile. "How about the paper though? Did you find it?"

Charles spoke this time. "We looked Father, but they're all out!"

The jolly-faced gentleman looked very curious upon hearing this. "Are you sure, young feller? Why we haven't had but a handful of customers all morning, and only a couple of 'em bought a paper."

Charles gulped. "P-positive," he stuttered. Meanwhile, Clara stared at her toes.

"Let's just go have a look then, Mr. Swope," said the gentleman, coming out from around the counter and guiding Father to the back of the store with a friendly hand upon his shoulder. "I'm sure we'll find one around here somewheres. I knows they can't all have been bought — stacked four or five of 'em in the rack m'self this mornin'!"

But, just as Charles had said, there was not a morning paper to be found. "Well I'll be a monkey's banan-er," said the man, scratching at his silver whiskers. "That right there ain't possible!"

"Really, it's quite alright," said Father, genially.

"No it ain't, Mr. Swope — it sure ain't. You here's a payin' customer, and yous come to buy yerself a paper, and I's the one tha's supposed to supply it. I've done yeh a disservice! I'm sure you never let such'er thing happen in yer little store, no-sir-ee!" he said, digging through the copies of *Harper's Magazine* and *Good Housekeeping* in hopes of unearthing a stray paper for Father.

"Truly, Mr. Tate, I'll manage," Father insisted. "There's never anything good in the paper anyway — I've just gotten into the habit of reading it, that's all," he said, though in truth he'd always found the paper rather stimulating.

"Yes," said Everett, pulling on his Father's shirt sleeve. "We should probably be getting back anyway. It looks as though it might rain."

Father glanced out the store window and cocked an eyebrow at his eldest son. "Whatever do you mean, my boy? It's perfectly sunny!"

Mr. Tate nodded. "They ain't callin' fer rain," he said. "Just heard the weather on the radio a bit ago." He retraced his steps back to the cash-register. "You know, Mr. Swope, just cause yous a special customer, I've an idea!"

"Have you?" said Father.

"Yes-sir-ee," said Mr. Tate, slipping back behind the counter. "I seems to think I left m'own copy of the paper behind here somewheres after I finished wid it this mornin'. I always read it, yeh see, while I'm havin' my cup'a orange juice. I'll sells yeh my copy! And at a discount cause it's be read!" He ducked below the counter and out of sight, and they could hear him fishing around in an attempt to unearth the aforementioned copy.

Everett grunted helplessly, and Charles moaned, and just as Mr. Tate's silver head popped back up from behind the counter, Clara uttered something that sounded very much like "Uhhah", and she promptly fainted, falling to the floor in a heap of tiny limbs and linen fabric.

"Clara!" shouted Father, and he bent down to scoop the girl up from the floor. "I'm sorry, Mr. Tate. I better rush her back home. I think she's fainted!"

"Yessum, yeh better! Golly, gee, I hope the poor little thing's alright! Good day to you, good day!" said Mr. Tate, dashing to the front of the store on a sprightly set of feet to hold the door open for them.

Father carried Clara out of the store and quickly made his way home with Charles and Everett at his heels. Though the boys were of course relieved that Father hadn't managed to obtain the paper, they'd never seen anybody faint before, and they found it quite worrying.

"Do you think she'll be alright?" asked Charles, bouncing on his toes to get a good view of Clara in his father's arms.

Father nodded. "She's breathing!" he grunted in reply.

A few moments later they burst in through the house, and Mother came running from the kitchen.

"My heavens, Edward! What's with all the commotion?" she said, but upon spotting the limp body of her niece in his arms, she cried out "Put her on the couch! What's happened?!"

Mother then grabbed a wet tea-towel as they filled her in, and when she began dabbing at Clara's pasty forehead, the girl finally rustled and her eyes flickered open.

"Clara, my dear, speak to me ... are you alright? You've given us a fright!" said Mother, still dabbing every inch of the girl's face with the towel.

At first, Clara could only mumble, but then she swallowed hard and said, "I'm fine! I just felt very f-faint all of a sudden, and I fell over. I'm *sorry*!" she cried, feeling as though she must have upset them terribly.

"No need to apologize!" said Father kindly, giving Clara's foot a squeeze from where he stood at the other end of the sofa. "Must've been the heat. Yesterday it was as chilly as a fall afternoon, and go figure, today there's a heat wave! That's Maryland for you!"

Mother then sent Father to fetch the cold compress, "And you boys stay here with Clara," she added. "I'm going to get her a glass of water."

Then, once the children were alone, Everett leaned in close to his cousin. "Alright, Clara. Be honest — you fainted on purpose, didn't you? That was *wicked* brilliant!"

"Wasn't it, though?!" said Clara, nodding her head eagerly and smiling. She and Everett both giggled, but Charles was looking befuddled.

"You mean you were only pretending?" he asked. "I was really worried!"

"Not *really* pretending," said Clara. "I felt like I was going to faint anyway, and then I thought I should probably stop myself, but I felt so very lightheaded, and I figured that it might distract Uncle Edward if I *did* faint, so then I thought *why not*? and everything went black! My knee hurts though from where I fell over," she said, rubbing at her leg and wincing.

Everett looked prouder than they'd ever seen him. "You're a mate, Clara!" he said, and he chucked her on the shoulder.

In Which The Swopes Go
For A Drive

We've come to the end of the things. Not the true end of things, because I've yet to tell you the *very* end, but the end of the children's adventures with the turban at least. They'd held a meeting in the nursery and unanimously decided to give the turban a rest (yes, even Everett) because they'd found magic much too tricky and complicated and had grown tired of all the trouble. Of course, this resolution did not last forever because magic is also very tempting, but I had to end the book somewhere, as I'm sure you'll agree, otherwise you might never get around to the other books piled upon your night stand, and the characters in those stories probably wouldn't like that very much. Everett in particular was rather miffed that I wasn't telling you about *all* their adventures, but that's only because he thinks everything that happens to him is interesting — he's *that* sort, you know. Nevertheless, I knew I had to end our story eventually, and what happened next seemed to be as good a place as any.

The day after the newspaper ordeal and Clara's fainting spell felt unusually calm. The children weren't being chased from a fair or race-track, and they weren't pushing a motorcar up a hill either, and Father was seated comfortably at the breakfast table reading a Watson-less morning newspaper. All was well, and their tummies were full from the French toast, eggs, bacon, and sausage Mother had made them. In fact, things were so relaxed that when the telephone rang in Father's stockroom, all three children nearly fell out of their seats.

Everyone exchanged curious glances, including Mother and Father, for the telephone had finally stopped ringing days ago and hadn't bothered them since. At its peak, it had gotten so bothersome that Father had taken to not answering it at all because he'd grown weary of telling people that they had the wrong number and had not reached the Coopstown Taxi Company as they'd hoped. On this morning however, Father felt oddly compelled to answer it, and it was a good thing he did.

"Oh, hello, Mr. Tate!" the children heard him shout down the telephone. At first they were concerned, suspecting that the man must be terribly persistent and had managed to locate a copy of the previous day's paper for Father, but it quickly became clear that he hadn't called about the newspaper at all, and instead about something entirely different.

"She's quite alright, thank you!" Father said in response to something the gentleman had asked. "Came-to the minute we got her home and laid her out on the couch. Probably just the heat — very kind of you to ask!"

Clara blushed at the memory of her fainting stunt, and Everett then nudged Charles, who was chewing his bacon much too loudly for them to properly hear Father's conversation.

"No, I'm afraid my days of owning a grocery store are over. Much too costly to re-build," they heard Father explain. "Work is hard to come by though."

There was then a long pause in which Father made several curious mumblings and responses, the likes of which only served to further confuse and frustrate those trying to listen in.

"You don't say," he said, but exactly what it was that Mr. Tate did or didn't say, the children still had no idea. "I'm honored, Mr. Tate, but how can you be certain? I mean, we only just met yesterday!"

Now the children were really curious, and even Mother had stopped what she was doing to pay closer attention. Though the conversation continued for only another few minutes, it felt more like a few hours for they still hadn't been able to fit the pieces together in their heads.

"You'll never believe what's just happened!" said Father, clapping his hands together victoriously upon re-entering the kitchen. He then planted a cheerful kiss on

Mother's cheek and scanned each of their faces, clearly expecting someone to attempt at least one good guess.

Charles bit his lip nervously. "They found your newspaper?" he said.

"Nope!" said Father. "Better than that!"

The children sighed in relief, and even without yet knowing what the good news was they suddenly felt quite as cheerful as Father.

"You've got a job?!" cried Mother hopefully, her arms braced for a celebratory hug.

"You're close!" said Father. "But it's even better than all that! Mr. Tate of Tate's grocery wants to retire to Florida to be near his children, and he's asked me to *run* his store! Can you believe it?!"

Mother wailed and leapt into Father's arms, tears of joy leaking from her eyes. "Oh, Edward! That's fantastic news!"

"Isn't it though?!" cried Father, now hugging each of the children, who thought they might all cry tears of joy too, for they loved seeing Mother and Father so happy. Of course, Everett and Charles weren't about to succumb to such excessive emotion *that* easily though, and they blinked several times until the urge had passed.

"Mr. Tate'll continue to check up on things from time to time, of course, but he said he's been looking for a means to retire for the past year!" continued Father, who was prone to rambling whenever he was really excited about something.

They were all so happy that Everett was surprised when a rather sad thought entered his head. "Father?" he said. "What about Watson?"

"Oh, right!" said Father with a snap of his fingers. "I almost forgot the best bit! I told Mr. Tate, I said — Mightn't you have need of a produce man? because I know just the person for the job! And he said that he'd never had a produce man before, but that that was probably why his produce always looked so peaked. So Watson's got a job too!"

"*Ohh*, let's go tell him!" cried Clara, jumping up and down on her toes. "He'll be so pleased!" Charles and Everett then followed her hurriedly up the stairs to Watson's bedroom, and Watson was indeed every bit as pleased as Mother and Father.

"Well, who'da thunk it! Steady work, huh? Now I can buy a new pair of overalls and some handkerchiefs!" he said, but the children told him that he ought to buy something really exciting, and not just something he needed, because now he'd be able to buy those things any day.

"When do we start, boss?" Watson asked Father once he and the children had come down the stairs and congregated in the kitchen.

"Effective immediately," said Father, slapping Watson heartily on the back. "Might as well get the hang of things — Mr. Tate leaves for Florida next week!"

"Can we go with you, Father?!" asked Everett.

"Now, children, we mustn't disturb——" began Mother, but Father quickly replied, "Why not?! We'll all go, and then you can be the first to thank Mr. Tate!"

"Hooray!" cried the children, and Mother simply smiled and shrugged her shoulders. "Best get your boots on then!" she told them. "I'll get baby Isabelle ready."

Soon everyone was stepping out the door and into the brilliant sunshine, and Mother opened her pretty pink parasol and swung it over her head so as to shade the baby from the sun. Father had told them to bring Poncho along too because he could do with an outing the same as the rest of them, and so Everett walked the dog on his lead, though in actuality Poncho was the one doing most of the walking and Everett was more or less dragged behind.

They'd barely made it past the mailbox when they heard the honking of a horn and turned to see The Man With The Very Large Mustache Indeed driving up the road in the old motorcar and waving to them from behind the wheel. They waved back eagerly, and he brought the car to a stop beside them on the road where it purred happily, almost as though it could tell how well its shiny gray hood looked on such a pleasant sunny day.

"Hiyah there, Swopes!" he called, leaning out the side of the car and grinning at them through the tufts of his mustache.

Father and Mother greeted him back, calling him by name, though it didn't sound any more familiar to the children this time than it had the first several times they'd heard it.

"So you got the car working again, did you?" said Everett to the man, quite forgetting that he wasn't supposed to know about its having died and needed pushing back up the hill.

"Of course! I told you kids the last time I saw yeh it'd been fixed! You haven't still been playing in it, have yeh?" said the man with the mustache.

All three children shook their heads (well, Charles and Everett shook theirs, and Clara sort of twitched), and they each felt their faces grow hot from a collective guilty conscience.

"Anyways, it ran out of gas somehow, but I've filled her back up and she's ready to go! 'Fraid she won't be goin' very far though," he said.

"Why's that?" asked Everett.

"Aye," he sighed, "my sale fell through! The man from Philadelphia t'was supposed to buy her says he's no longer interested. Apparently he's decided this drivin' thing's just a fad, and so he figures he'll invest in zippers instead."

"Zippers?" repeated Charles.

"Yep," grunted the man with the mustache. "They're for clothes — slides up and down the fronts of mens' trousers and the backs of ladies' dresses and things. Supposed to replace buttons, they say."

"Huh!" said each of the Swopes (and Clara) with interest, for though *you* may have zippers on all of your trousers and dresses, back in 1920 they'd only just been thought of.

"Where y'all need to get?" said the man. "I'll sell yeh this here car to do the gettin'!"

Father bent his head back in a hearty laugh. "Well, Watson and I have just been offered a job running Tate's Grocery in town," Father began to explain.

"Somethin' happen to Old Mr. Tate?" asked the mustached man.

"Nope! Nothing besides wanting a little peace and quiet in Florida. He's retiring!" said Father.

"Well, then!" cried the man, giving the steering wheel a firm slap. "You'll be wanting a car to drive back and forth to work, won't yeh?"

Father laughed again, although this time a little less heartily and a little more as though he were thinking at the same time. "Oh, I don't know ... it's not that long a walk, really. And you know what they say — don't count your chickens before they've hatched!"

"But I'll sell it to you on credit! You can pay me in installments. Truth is, I could use the money, and the poor old thing's just been sittin' out in the field for the last year or so — I'm sure it'd appreciate the use."

"Hmm," said Father in thought, chewing on his bottom lip and momentarily ignoring Everett and Charles's persistent tugging upon his shirt sleeve.

"We'll keep it clean and polished for you Father, and Everett knows how to start the car with that hand crank thingy on the front!" said Charles.

"Does he, now?" said Father curiously.

Everett growled under his breath at his younger brother, and Charles quickly amended his statement. "Come to think of it, I think he was only pretending," Charles grumbled.

"Go on, Father!" goaded Everett.

"No strings attached!" the man with the mustache chimed in. "If yeh can't make the payments, I'll just buy it back and try my luck elsewhere. But I'd rather yer nice family have it than anybody else — I *do* love the old girl, you know," he said, running his hands affectionately along the steering wheel. "So how about it, Mr. Swope?"

Both the boys and Clara nodded eagerly at Father, and Mother had that special glint in her eye that she always got when she knew what Father was thinking before he'd even thought it, and finally he said, "Well, alright! I do miss having a car. You have a deal, Mr. ——" and Father said the man's name again, but it had so many letters and they were in such funny places that even *I* couldn't catch enough of them to write it down for you.

Father gave the man with the mustache a modest down payment with the promise of more to come, and soon they were driving down the road in the car and waving goodbye to him and shouting "Thank you!" over and over again. Father, Mother and baby Isabelle were in the front seat, Charles, Everett and Watson were in the back seat, and Poncho was panting happily behind them in the rumble seat next to Clara, whom, I might add, immediately spotted the hidden newspapers at her feet, and threw them over the side of the car with a pronounced yipe.

"You know, Everett," began Father, turning his head slightly to address his elder son. "I've just remembered — one of the ladies I mow lawns for was telling me the other day that she'd received a ride from a rather short taxi driver last week. Said the fellow was a dead ringer for *you*! Quite comical, isn't it," said Father, jovially.

Everett forced a laugh. "That's really funny, Father," he said, suddenly feeling queazy. "Which lady was it?"

"A Missus Brown," replied Father. "Used to come into the store sometimes for the gossip papers, though she always told me they were for a sick friend."

"Hmm, I've never heard of her before," said Everett as innocently as possible. "Have *you*, Charles?" he added uncomfortably, turning to his brother.

"No. Never," said Charles, dutifully.

"Nor have I!" said Clara, wanting to help, but Charles and Everett both rolled their eyes, for Clara couldn't possibly have encountered Mrs. Brown in Father's store anyway seeing as it had burned down a half a year before she'd even arrived.

"Oh, look," said Father, now pointing and waving to a plump woman wearing a straw hat who'd just stepped out her front door. "It's Missus Whimpole! I mow *her* lawn on Thursdays."

"Do you?" said Mother politely.

The children gasped and crouched down low in their seats, praying that Father wouldn't stop to talk, which he might have done if he hadn't been distracted by their curious reaction.

"Whatever's the matter with you three?" he asked. "I know you were much taller than that a minute ago. Why are you crouching?"

"Uhh ..." said Everett with a gulp and a peek over the side of the car.

"Erm," mumbled Clara, sinking even lower in her seat.

"T-there was a *bee!*" Charles quickly exclaimed. "Buzzing about our heads!"

"Yes!" Clara added. "It was big and fat with yellow and black stripes!"

"Was it, now?" said Father in amusement.

"I didn't see no bee," muttered Watson, gazing up above his head.

"Don't swat at it," said Mother with a hint of concern. "Bees are just as afraid of us as we are of them," she added, which must be in some handbook on mothering because I'm sure we've *all* been told this by our mothers at one time or another.

Feeling as though there was now a sufficient distance between the car and Mrs. Whimpole, the children straightened themselves back up in their seats and soon spotted Tate's Grocery just a little ways farther up the street.

Father parked their new motorcar along the curb outside the store and took baby Isabelle from Mother as she stepped out of the car, followed closely by the children and Poncho who'd all hopped out of the back seat. Poncho, to his great disappointment, was then tied up to a lamp post and given a consoling pat on the head and a doggy biscuit, the latter having at least taken the sting off his abandonment.

"I'll get the door for you, Mother!" offered Charles, jumping ahead to yank it open, and Mr. Tate, who had been behind the counter, leapt out to greet them upon hearing the welcoming jingle emitted by the door.

"Why, Mr. Swope! It's so good ter see ya!" he said, extending a callused hand out for Father to shake. "And this here must be yer fam'ly! Missus Swope, I presume?" he said to Mother, taking her hand in his to kiss.

Mother blushed. "Yes, sir, Mr. Tate. We're awfully grateful for your kindness to Edward and Watson," she said, letting her eyes take in the surroundings.

"We're grateful too!" said Everett, and both Charles and Clara then made similar declarations so as not to be left out.

"Well, yer father's doin' me a great big favor!" Mr. Tate told them with a smile. "I got chil'ren of m'own, yeh see, and some gran' chil'ren too! But I don't get to see much of 'em up here, so I'm mighty anxious to get down south and spend some good ol' fashioned qual'ty time wid 'em!"

Mr. Tate was then introduced to Watson, whom he greeted warmly with a firm handshake and the sentiment that he was "mighty" relieved at knowing his customers wouldn't have to suffer through any more bruised apples or squished bananas with Watson on the payroll.

Unlike the day before, the store was now full of customers scattered throughout the aisles, and with several claps of his hands and a call of "Listen up, folks!", Mr. Tate had acquired everyone's attention. A dozen or more faces now stared quizzically at the grocery store owner and then at the Swope family, and nobody, the Swopes included, had any idea what Mr. Tate was about to say.

"I've an announcement," he said, plopping an arm around Father's shoulder. "All God's chil'ren gets to be an age when they can no longer do as much as they used ter, and they needs to call it a day and pass on the torch. I've been in the grocery business for some thirty-five years, but now it's time for me to embrace m'old age and spend some time with m'loved ones. That's why you're lookin' at the new boss of Tate's grocery right here," he said, thumping Father on the back. "Edward Swope! And I'd like ter welcome our new head of produce, Mr. Watson ... uh," he looked to Watson to supply the rest of his name.

"Harris!" said Watson with a grateful nod.

"Mr. Watson Harris, folks! Welcome, welcome. I'm proud to be passing on my duties to such qualified gentleman." Mr. Tate then began to clap with gusto, and the customers politely followed suit, several of them coming up to greet Father, Mother, Watson and the children, or to coo over baby Isabelle.

Two gentlemen who'd once been regulars at Father's store were busy telling Father, Mother and Watson some town gossip when the children thought they'd overheard one of the men mention the name Barney Lucas. Now, if you remember, the man whom Charles and Everett had always referred to as "Mean Old Barney Lucas" was the same man who had caused such a stink about Watson in the beginning of our story, and it had always been suspected that he was indeed underneath one of those white hoods the night Father's grocery store was burned down. You'll probably also remember that I told you you'd be sorely disappointed if you were hoping this story would end with each of the white-hooded figures in handcuffs, and unfortunately that is still true ... but there was one exception.

"I say! The man's an imbecile!" exclaimed one of the gentlemen, still speaking of Barney Lucas. "Got himself fired by Mr. Cooper for his racist ranting, and then he tried to rough up one of Mr. Cooper's black workers! That's when Mr. Cooper shot him in the foot and called the police. Had him arrested for public endangerment! Apparently other charges against him are now coming out of the woodwork — it's likely he won't see daylight for quite some time. And Mr. Cooper's gunshot blew off two of his toes, they say!"

Charles and Everett felt rather giddy with vindication upon hearing this, though they weren't sure if it was quite right of them to feel so glad of Mr. Lucas's two missing toes. Everett, however, said that he thought two toes was a small price to pay for how Mr. Lucas had treated Watson, and for what he'd done to Father's store. "And besides," he added, "he brought it on himself."

Mother, Father and Watson were all taking in this bit of news, and Clara was badgering Charles and Everett about Mr. Lucas, whom she'd never heard of, when all of a sudden Mr. Tate came and pulled the children aside.

213

"Listen here," he said, gently huddling them together. "I have this feelin' I've seen that feller before." The children followed Mr. Tate's outstretched finger to see that it was pointing straight at Watson. "Is he famous or somethin'? I can't put my finger on it, but it's been buggin' me ever since I laid eyes on 'im."

Everett, Charles and Clara all blinked and looked to one another to say something, only each of them was as silent as the next.

Mr. Tate's eyes darted from one face to the other, and in receiving no answer he bent his head back and gaped at the ceiling looking ponderous. Everett was just about to mutter a flimsy denial of Mr. Tate's suspicions when the man suddenly snapped his fingers. "Ah ha!" he said. "You know, come to think of it, he looks mighty like that Underchief from the bank or what-not that was in the paper yester'dy. *Yes-sir-ee*, I think that's where I seen him!"

"Oh, you mustn't say anything!" begged Clara, grasping her hands together as if in prayer.

"Why ever not?" asked Mr. Tate vehemently, but certainly not meanly.

Always the quickest thinker of the bunch, Charles motioned for Mr. Tate to bend down to his level, and once the man had obliged, the boy cupped a hand to his ear. "That was his twin brother, but they're en*strangled* and he doesn't like to talk about it," Charles said in a whisper.

"Oh, I see," said Mr. Tate with a knowing nod. "Don't worry yerselves then, it'll be our little secret! I knows all about dem fam'ly squabbles!"

"Oh, you *are* a dear!" said Clara tearfully, and she leapt to hug Mr. Tate, though she could only manage a little squeeze around his waist for he was very tall.

He bellowed in laughter and squeezed her back, and then Father and Watson approached them looking very pleased to see Mr. Tate and the children getting on so well.

"We're ready to get started!" said Father eagerly, clapping his hands together. "What'll it be first, Mr. Tate?"

The man beamed at them. "Well, I wonder if you two might help me with somethin' ... there was a spill back in the cleanin' aisle, and I can't get down on the floor like I used ter. But there's no telling what you might find down there — hasn't had a proper sweep through in ages. With m'eyesight, I can't see the dirt ter sweep it!"

Father and Watson were happy to be put to use so quickly, and Mother then began to herd the children toward the door with her Isabelle-free hand. "Come now — let's leave Father and Watson to their work," she said.

The children then waved eagerly and called out "Goodbye, Father! Goodbye, Watson! Goodbye, Mr. Tate — have a good life in Florida!" and Mr. Tate returned the wave and gave them a wink.

"Alright now, come along dears," said Mother kindly, ushering them out the door.

"Can *you* drive us home, Mother?" asked Charles.

"No, we'll walk," Mother replied. "Your father says women lack the necessary faculties to drive," she muttered icily, "though we'll just see about that! But today's not the day to prove him wrong. Everett — you fetch Poncho."

Their snowy white friend was drooling and wagging his fluffy tail back and forth with boundless energy when Everett untied him from the lamp post and struggled to remain upright as the dog yanked against the confines of his lead. "Steady there, boy!" Everett yelped, but Poncho dragged him the entire length of the way home nevertheless.

"Isn't it wonderful?" Clara gushed to Charles and Everett once they were back inside the house and out of earshot, seeing as Mother had gone to change baby Isabelle's nappy. "Uncle Edward and Watson have jobs, and we never have to see that turban again if we don't wish!"

Charles and Everett had to agree that everything had indeed worked out nicely.

"Thank goodness Father never saw that paper!" said Charles.

But instead of agreeing, Clara clapped a hand over her mouth. "Oh, no!" she cried. "I've just had a thought!"

"What?!" said both Charles and Everett insistently.

"Well, if Uncle Edward and Watson are now working at the grocery store ..." she began.

"And *we* put the newspapers behind those tins ..." Charles continued, now adopting the same worried expression that had inflicted his cousin.

"Oh, bother!" cried Everett, and before any of them could say another word, they'd leapt to their feet and scrambled back out the door ...

And now, dear readers, comes the time for me to bid you farewell. I could keep going of course, but I do hate it when books tie up everything with pretty ribbons and bows in the end, because everyone knows that life is not comprised of limitless ribbons and bows, but of adventure and excitement, which never truly ends. For those of you wondering if Father and Watson ever did see that newspaper that day, I will tell you that Clara never shed a tear, and therefore whatever happened couldn't

216

have been all that bad. Though, if there's a lesson to be learned, it would be this: If a mischievous uncle (especially the dead, former member of the aristocracy kind) ever sends you a trunk in the mail ... don't open it.

The Very End

About The Illustrator

Lindsey Loegters received her design degree from Miami University of Ohio in 2002. She currently works as a freelance designer and illustrator in Chicago, IL. She is also the illustrator of the children's novel, *Giggleswick*. If you'd like to see more of her work, please visit her website at www.lindseyloegters.com

Look for Matthew Mainster's first book for children, *Giggleswick*, in print & e-book formats!

Visit the Official Giggleswick site at
http://theworldofgiggleswick.blogspot.com/

Visit Matthew Mainster on facebook at
http://www.facebook.com/MatthewMainster

Join the Giggleswick fan-club! Visit
http://www.facebook.com/pages/Giggleswick/148178561975784